SHORT STORIES

by

CHARLES DICKENS

Other titles in the Thornes Classic series

Short Stories (Series Editor: Mike Royston)

Hans Christian Andersen (edited by Sarah Matthews and Mike Royston)
Arthur Conan Doyle (edited by Sarah Matthews)
Thomas Hardy (edited by Mike Royston)
Katherine Mansfield (edited by Mike Royston)
Guy de Maupassant (edited by Mike Royston)
Edgar Allan Poe (edited by Mike Royston)
H. G. Wells (edited by Mike Royston)
Oscar Wilde (edited by Mike Royston)

Novels (Series Editor: John Seely)

The Adventures of Huckleberry Finn by Mark Twain (edited by Sarah Matthews)
A Christmas Carol and *The Cricket on the Hearth* by Charles Dickens
     (edited by Frank Green)
Gulliver's Travels by Jonathan Swift (edited by Huw Parker)
The Lost World by Arthur Conan Doyle (edited by Sarah Matthews)
Pride and Prejudice by Jane Austen (edited by Andrew Worrall)
The Red Badge of Courage by Stephen Crane (edited by Frank Green)
Silas Marner by George Eliot (edited by Elizabeth Seely)
The Strange Case of Dr Jekyll and Mr Hyde and *The Beach of Falesá* by Robert
     Louis Stevenson (edited by John Seely)
The Turn of the Screw by Henry James (edited by Paul Roberts)
Wuthering Heights by Emily Brontë (edited by Elizabeth Seely)

Also

Classic Poetry: A practical guide for Key Stage 3 (edited by John Foster and
     Gordon Dennis)
Classic Poetry 2: A practical guide for Key Stage 4 (edited by John Foster and
     Gordon Dennis)

Thornes Classic Short Stories

SHORT STORIES

by
CHARLES DICKENS

EDITED BY MIKE ROYSTON

SERIES EDITOR: MIKE ROYSTON

Stanley Thornes (Publishers) Ltd

The Signalman first published 1866
Confession Found in a Prison first published 1842
The Trial for Murder first published 1865
The Hanged Man's Bride first published 1860

This edition first published in 1997 by:
Stanley Thornes (Publishers) Ltd
Ellenborough House
Wellington Street
CHELTENHAM GL50 1YW
England

97 98 99 00 01 / 10 9 8 7 6 5 4 3 2 1

A catalogue record for this book is available from the British Library.

ISBN 0–7487–3095–8

Acknowledgements

The author and publishers are grateful to the following for permission to reproduce illustrations and photographs:
Mary Evans Picture Library p. 6 (bottom) ● The Trustees of Dickens House Museum, Chatham, pp. 2 (both), 3 (both), 4, 5 (both).

Typeset by Tech-Set, Gateshead
Illustrated by Dick Barton
With thanks to Sue Whimster for her editorial work on this book.
Printed and bound in Great Britain at T J Press (Padstow) Ltd, Cornwall

Contents

How to use this book   1

Introduction:

    About the writer   2
    Background to the stories   5
    Other recommended stories by Charles Dickens   7

The stories:

    The Signalman   9
     Study guide   24

    Confession Found in a Prison   31
     Study guide   39

    The Trial for Murder   43
     Study guide   56

    The Hanged Man's Bride   61
     Study guide   81

Overview:

    Extended Study guide   85

How to use this book

This book contains four short stories by Charles Dickens. It is designed so that you can read the stories on your own, or share your reading with others. Whichever way you read, the stories have been chosen above all to be *enjoyed*.

The Introduction contains:

- a brief account of the writer's life. This gives you an impression of the kind of person he was and outlines the most important things that happened to him during his lifetime.

- a background to the stories, in words and pictures. This tells you about the kind of stories they are and helps you to approach your reading of them in an informed way.

To help you get the most from them, the stories have been presented in a particular way. They contain the following features:

- boxes at the beginning of each story, and at other key points, which suggest what you should look out for as you read;

- a glossary at the foot of every page giving the meanings of words you may find unfamiliar;

- a commentary summarising what is happening on each page of the story, to help you follow it as you read.

During each story, you will now and again come across a 'Pause for playback' section. This contains brief questions to highlight important points in the part of the story you have just read. You can make up your own mind about the 'answers'. They do not have to be written down.

After each story, there is a Study guide. This contains activities designed to help you form an understanding of the story as a whole. Some activities are for small groups, some are for pairs, and some for doing by yourself.

At the end of the book, you will find an Overview section. This asks you to think further about how the stories are written and to make some comparisons between them.

Enjoy your reading!

Introduction

ABOUT THE WRITER

In his best-known novels – *David Copperfield*, for example, or *Great Expectations* – Dickens writes so intensely about childhood that he seems to be re-living it. This is not surprising. His own early years were so full of upheaval and uncertainty that they left a deep impression, not to say a deep scar, on his mind.

Charles Dickens was born near Portsmouth in 1812, the second child of a middle-class family. His father, John, was a Navy pay clerk. The more children John Dickens produced – there were finally eight in all – the more incapable he became of providing for them. The family fell into serious debt. In 1824, when Charles was barely 12, his father was declared bankrupt and sent to the dreaded Marshalsea Prison for debtors in London.

Dickens at the age of 40

His wife and the other children lived in the prison too. Charles, however, did not. He was taken from school and sent, aged 12, to work in Warren's

The courtyard of the Marshalsea Prison

'blacking' factory. He was employed in the warehouse, labelling bottles of paste intended to shine shoes. After work, he returned to his nearby lodgings, where he lived in semi-squalor in an attic room.

Dickens escaped Warren's when his father, typically, borrowed money to send him to a private school. But the Wellington House Academy taught him little: the masters were savage and the academic standards low. By the age of 15, Dickens was working again: first as a clerk for a Law firm, then as a freelance reporter on legal matters in the Doctors' Commons near St Paul's. For hour after hour, he scribbled down rambling legal arguments about wills and testaments. This tedium lasted four years.

Having taught himself shorthand, Dickens finally became a journalist reporting on business in the House of Commons.

Dickens's time at Warren's 'blacking' factory haunted him all his life

His apprenticeship as a reporter stood him in good stead. Using the pen-name 'Boz', he began to publish accounts (or 'Sketches') of London life in various magazines. Then, in 1836–7, he brought out in serial form *The Pickwick Papers*. It was such a success that Dickens could, in his mid-twenties, afford to become a full-time writer of novels and stories.

His output was enormous, from *Oliver Twist* (1837) to *Our Mutual Friend* (1865). Dickens's appetite for writing, and his enjoyment of his own popularity, led him to edit several periodicals, notably *Household Words* (later *All The Year Round*) in which his short stories were published. He had an equal appetite for life. He married Catherine Hogarth in 1836, had nine children by her, and separated from her in 1858. This gave rise to a public scandal about Dickens's 'improper' relationship with the actress Ellen Ternan.

A painting of Catherine Hogarth in about 1846

Over-work killed him. Having bought a country house – Gad's Hill Place, near Rochester in Kent – in 1856, Dickens did anything but 'retire' to it. Instead he undertook a number of exhausting Public Reading tours to which audiences all over the country flocked to hear him read from his own books. Drained and suffering from stress, he died suddenly of a stroke in 1870 at the age of 56. He is buried in Poet's Corner in Westminster Abbey.

Gad's Hill Place – Dickens is strolling in the garden

BACKGROUND TO THE STORIES

Christmas ghosts

When Dickens published *A Christmas Carol: A Ghost Story for Christmas* in 1843, he could not have guessed what he was starting. Quite simply, it became the best-known, and best-loved, ghost story ever written. Even today there is hardly anyone who gets past childhood without knowing about its villain–hero, Scrooge, haunted into being a reformed character by Marley's Ghost and three seasonal spirits.

A *Christmas Carol* was hugely popular with Victorian readers – so much so that, for the rest of his life, Dickens usually brought out a 'ghost story' at the end of the year. Very few of them are about Christmas but they *are* about the supernatural. Four of the best are printed in this volume.

An illustration from the first edition of A Christmas Carol

Dickens's magazines

In 1850, Dickens began the 'twopenny weekly' *Journal* (or magazine) *Household Words*, renamed *All the Year Round* nine years later. He remained its editor until his death. In it, he published his *Christmas Stories* – some of them written with his close friend Wilkie Collins, but most by himself. All the stories in this book first appeared there or in the short-lived journal also edited by Dickens, *Master Humphrey's Clock*.

'Winter stories'

For Dickens, a Christmas story *was* a ghost story. It was an English tradition, and few Victorians had a stronger sense of tradition than Dickens. This is how he pictures his own family in *The Christmas Tree* (1850): 'We are telling

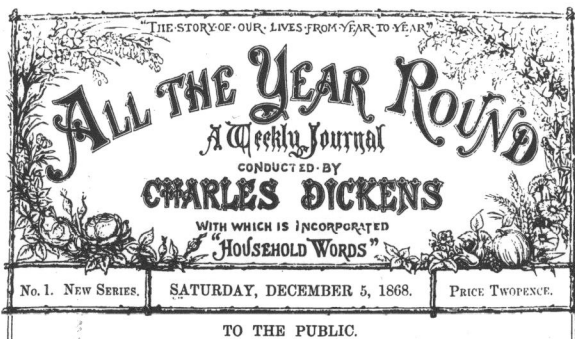

A title page from All the Year Round, *in which Dickens published his Christmas stories*

The spirit of a Dickensian Christmas

winter stories – Ghost Stories, or more shame for us – round the Christmas fire; and we have never stirred, except to draw a little nearer to it.' One hundred and fifty years later, we are more likely to be sitting near a radiator watching videos. The stories in this book may help you decide which sort of entertainment *you* would prefer.

Dickens and the supernatural

Dickens had a strong interest in the occult. He attended séances, paid frequent visits to demonstrations of hypnotism ('mesmerism', as the Victorians called it), and was an effective hypnotist himself. In particular, he believed in the power of dreams to predict the future – something, he claimed, which occurred in his own life many times. As for ghosts: 'I have always had a strong interest in the subject', he said, 'and never lose an opportunity of pursuing it.'

This lifelong fascination with the supernatural may explain why Dickens is considered by many to be a spellbinding teller of ghost stories. The ones in this book will allow you to judge for yourself.

The ghost of an idea

As you will discover, the themes of Dickens's stories go well beyond the supernatural. Like all his fiction, they are about good and evil, justice and injustice, meanness and generosity, love and hate. The stories are populated by ghosts – but the ghosts

The gruesome side of Victorian life: murder was rife, as three stories in this volume show

are, more often than not, a means of exploring the ideas that most interested their author. Above all, the stories are meant to *entertain*. As Dickens, the great entertainer of English literature, wrote in the preface to *A Christmas Carol*:

> 'I have endeavoured, in this Ghostly little book, to raise the Ghost of an Idea, which shall not put my readers out of humour with themselves, with the season, or with me. May it haunt their houses pleasantly.'

OTHER RECOMMENDED STORIES BY CHARLES DICKENS

The Black Veil

The Drunkard's Death

Tom Tiddler's Ground

The Poor Relation's Story

The Schoolboy's Story

The Seven Poor Travellers

The Haunted House

Mr Testator's Visitation

A Message from the Sea*

The Wreck of the Golden Mary*

(* written jointly with Wilkie Collins)

You can find these stories in *Christmas Stories* (Oxford, 1992) and *Sketches by Boz* (Penguin, 1995).

THE SIGNALMAN

Look out for…
- **the signalman's reactions to the story-teller when he first meets him.**
- **how the scenery around the signal-box is described: what sort of atmosphere do these descriptions create?**
- **whether you find anything unusual about what the signalman says/does.**

'Halloa! Below there!'

When he heard a voice thus calling to him, he was standing at the door of his box, with a flag in his hand, furled round its short pole. One would have thought, considering the nature of the ground, that he could not have doubted from what quarter the voice came; but instead of looking up to where I stood on the top of the steep cutting nearly over his head, he turned about and looked down the Line. There was something remarkable in his manner of doing so, though I could not have said for my life what. But I know it was remarkable enough to attract my notice, even though his figure was foreshortened and shadowed, down into the deep trench, and mine was high above him, so steeped in the glow of an angry sunset, that I had shaded my eyes with my hand before I saw him at all.

'Halloa! Below!'

From looking down the Line, he turned himself about again, and, raising his eyes, saw my figure high above him.

COMMENTARY

One evening, the story-teller comes to a railway line running through a very steep gorge. A signalman, standing outside his box, appears not to hear the story-teller greet him. Instead, he turns in the opposite direction and gazes down the line.

quarter: direction
cutting: narrow gorge
foreshortened: made to look smaller (and so further away)

'Is there any path by which I can come down and speak to you?'

He looked up at me without replying, and I looked down at him without pressing him too soon with a repetition of my idle question. Just then there came a vague vibration in the earth and air, quickly changing into a violent pulsation, and an oncoming rush that caused me to start back, as though it had the force to draw me down. When such vapour as rose to my height from this rapid train had passed me, and was skimming away over the landscape, I looked down again, and saw him refurling the flag he had shown while the train went by.

I repeated my inquiry. After a pause, during which he seemed to regard me with fixed attention, he motioned with his rolled-up flag towards a point on my level, some two or three hundred yards distant.

I called down to him, 'All right!' and made for that point. There, by dint of looking closely about me, I found a rough zigzag descending path notched out, which I followed.

The cutting was extremely deep, and unusually precipitate. It was made through a clammy stone, that became oozier and wetter as I went down. For these reasons, I found the way long enough to give me time to recall a singular air of reluctance or compulsion with which he had pointed out the path.

When I came down low enough upon the zigzag descent to see him again, I saw that he was standing between the rails on the way by which the train had lately passed, in an attitude as if he were waiting for me to appear. He had his left hand at his chin, and his left elbow rested on his right hand, crossed over his breast. His attitude was one of such expectation and watchfulness that I stopped a moment, wondering at it.

I resumed my downward way, and stepping out upon the level of the railroad, and drawing nearer to him, saw that he was a dark sallow man, with a dark beard and rather heavy eyebrows. His post was in as solitary and dismal a place as ever I saw. On either side, a dripping-wet wall of jagged stone, excluding all view but a strip of sky; the perspective one way only a crooked prolongation of this great dungeon; the shorter perspective in the other

idle: casual
violent pulsation: earth-shaking shudder
vapour: steam
by dint of: by means of
precipitate: steep
singular air: striking impression
attitude: posture, way of standing
post: place of work
prolongation: continuation

COMMENTARY
A train hurtles by. The signalman shows it his flag, indicating 'All clear' to the driver. Finally, he points out to the story-teller a path down to the line. The story-teller finds the signalman standing between the rails, staring at him intently.

direction terminating in a gloomy red light, and the gloomier entrance to a black tunnel, in whose massive architecture there was a barbarous, depressing, and forbidding air. So little sunlight ever found its way to this spot, that it had an earthy, deadly smell; and so much cold wind rushed through it, that it struck chill to me, as if I had left the natural world.

Before he stirred, I was near enough to him to have touched him. Not even then removing his eyes from mine, he stepped back one step, and lifted his hand.

This was a lonesome post to occupy (I said), and it had riveted my attention when I looked down from up yonder. A visitor was a rarity, I should suppose; not an unwelcome rarity, I hoped? In me, he merely saw a man who had been shut up within narrow limits all his life, and who, being at last set free, had a newly awakened interest in these great works. To such purpose I spoke to him; but I am far from sure of the terms I used; for, besides that I am not happy in opening any conversation, there was something in the man that daunted me.

He directed a most curious look towards the red light near the tunnel's mouth, and looked all about it, as if something were missing from it, and then looked at me.

That light was part of his charge? Was it not?

He answered in a low voice, 'Don't you know it is?'

The monstrous thought came into my mind, as I perused the fixed eyes and the saturnine face, that this was a spirit, not a man. I have speculated since, whether there may have been infection in his mind.

In my turn, I stepped back. But in making the action, I detected in his eyes some latent fear of me. This put the monstrous thought into flight.

'You look at me,' I said, forcing a smile, 'as if you had a dread of me.'

'I was doubtful,' he returned, 'whether I had seen you before.'

'Where?'

He pointed to the red light he had looked at.

'There?' I said.

Intently watchful of me, he replied (but without sound), 'Yes.'

COMMENTARY

The surroundings in which the signalman works are dark and solitary, like a prison. The signalman divides his attention between the story-teller's face and the red signal light at the opening of the tunnel. He seems unwilling to talk, as if he has some burden on his mind.

terminating: ending
barbarous: inhuman, uncivilised
great works: e.g. railways
daunted: overawed, frightened
charge: a responsibility of his job
perused: studied
saturnine: dark and gloomy
latent: hidden, suppressed

'My good fellow, what should I do there? However, be that as it may, I never was there, you may swear.'

'I think I may,' he rejoined. 'Yes; I am sure I may.'

His manner cleared, like my own. He replied to my remarks with readiness, and in well-chosen words. Had he much to do there? Yes; that was to say, he had enough responsibility to bear; but exactness and watchfulness were what was required of him, and of actual work – manual labour – he had next to none. To change that signal, to trim those lights, and to turn this iron handle now and then, was all he had to do under that head. Regarding those many long and lonely hours of which I seemed to make so much, he could only say that the routine of his life had shaped itself into that form, and he had grown used to it. He had taught himself a language down here – if only to know it by sight, and to have formed his own crude ideas of its pronunciation, could be called learning it. He had also worked at fractions and decimals, and tried a little algebra; but he was, and had been as a boy, a poor hand at figures. Was it necessary for him when on duty always to remain in that channel of damp air, and could he never rise into the sunshine from between those high stone walls? Why, that depended upon times and circumstances. Under some conditions there would be less upon the Line than under others, and the same held good as to certain hours of the day and night. In bright weather, he did choose occasions for getting a little above these lower shadows; but, being at all times liable to be called by his electric bell, and at such times listening for it with redoubled anxiety, the relief was less than I would suppose.

He took me into his box, where there was a fire, a desk for an official book in which he had to make certain entries, a telegraphic instrument with its dial, face, and needles, and the little bell of which he had spoken. On my trusting that he would excuse the remark that he had been well educated, and (I hoped I might say without offence), perhaps educated above that station, he observed that instances of slight incongruity in such wise would rarely be found wanting among large bodies of men; that he had heard it was so in the workhouses, in the police force, even in that last desperate resource, the army;

rejoined: answered
trim: keep the oil lamp in the signal-light burning
under that head: of that kind
poor hand: bad scholar
held good: remained true
bell: to warn him that a train is due
above that station: beyond what is required to be a signalman
incongruity in such wise: mismatch between a man's qualifications and his job

COMMENTARY
The signalman wonders if he has seen the story-teller before, at the mouth of the tunnel. Once he is convinced this is impossible, he relaxes and talks freely about his job. He has to stay alert at all times to change the signal for approaching trains.

and that he knew it was so, more or less, in any great railway staff. He had been, when young (if I could believe it, sitting in that hut – he scarcely could), a student of natural philosophy, and had attended lectures; but he had run wild, misused his opportunities, gone down, and never risen again. He had no complaint to offer about that. He had made his bed, and he lay upon it. It was far too late to make another.

All that I have here condensed he said in a quiet manner, with his grave dark regards divided between me and the fire. He threw in the word, 'Sir', from time to time, and especially when he referred to his youth – as though to request me to understand that he claimed to be nothing but what I found him. He was several times interrupted by the little bell, and had to read off messages, and send replies. Once he had to stand without the door, and display a flag as a train passed, and make some verbal communication to the driver. In the discharge of his duties, I observed him to be remarkably exact and vigilant, breaking off his discourse at a syllable, and remaining silent until what he had to do was done.

In a word, I should have set this man down as one of the safest of men to be employed in that capacity, but for the circumstance that while he was speaking to me he twice broke off with a fallen colour, turned his face towards the little bell when it did NOT ring, opened the door of the hut (which was kept shut to exclude the unhealthy damp), and looked out towards the red light near the mouth of the tunnel. On both of those occasions, he came back to the fire with the inexplicable air upon him which I had remarked, without being able to define, when we were so far asunder.

Said I, when I rose to leave him, 'You almost make me think that I have met with a contented man.'

(I am afraid that I must acknowledge that I said it to lead him on.)

'I believe I used to be so,' he rejoined, in the low voice in which he had first spoken; 'but I am troubled, Sir, I am troubled.'

He would have recalled the words if he could. He had said them, however, and I took them up quickly.

COMMENTARY

Inside the box, the signalman relates his life history. In youth he was a college student but 'ran wild' and wasted his chances. Now, he says, he is satisfied with the job he has. The story-teller notices that he twice glances at his bell when it does not ring.

natural philosophy: the study of nature
grave dark regards: solemn glances
without: outside
vigilant: watchful, alert
discourse: conversation
a fallen colour: a pale, anxious face
asunder: apart
recalled: taken back

'With what? What is your trouble?'

'It is very difficult to impart, Sir. It is very, very difficult to speak of. If ever you make me another visit, I will try to tell you.'

'But I expressly intend to make you another visit. Say, when shall it be?'

'I go off early in the morning, and I shall be on again at ten o'clock tomorrow night, Sir.'

'I will come at eleven.'

He thanked me, and went out at the door with me. 'I'll show my white light, Sir,' he said, in his peculiar low voice, 'till you have found the way up. When you have found it, don't call out! And when you are at the top, don't call out!'

His manner seemed to make the place strike colder to me, but I said no more than, 'Very well'.

'And when you come down tomorrow night, don't call out! Let me ask you a parting question. What made you cry out "Halloa! Below there!" tonight?'

PAUSE FOR PLAYBACK:

Now look at the playback questions on page 24 before going on with your reading.

Look out for...
- **the reasons why the signalman is so 'troubled'.**
- **how a sense of the supernatural grows stronger as the story develops.**
- **why the words 'Below there!' turn out to be of such importance to the story as a whole.**

---

impart: convey
expressly: certainly, specifically

COMMENTARY

It is late, and the story-teller gets up to go. The signalman suddenly confides that he is 'troubled' by something that is hard to explain. He seems particularly disturbed by the phrase 'Halloa! Below there!'

'Heaven knows,' said I. 'I cried something to that effect – '

'Not to that effect, Sir. Those were the very words. I know them well.'

'I admit those were the very words. I said them, no doubt, because I saw you below.'

'For no other reason?'

'What other reason could I possibly have?'

'You had no feeling that they were conveyed to you in any supernatural way?'

'No.'

He wished me good night, and held up his light. I walked by the side of the down Line of rails (with a very disagreeable sensation of a train coming behind me) until I found the path. It was easier to mount than to descend, and I got back to my inn without any adventure.

Punctual to my appointment, I placed my foot on the first notch of the zigzag next night, as the distant clocks were striking eleven. He was waiting for me at the bottom, with his white light on. 'I have not called out,' I said, when we came close together; 'may I speak now?' 'By all means, Sir.' 'Good night, then, and here's my hand.' 'Good night, Sir, and here's mine.' With that we walked side by side to his box, entered it, closed the door, and sat down by the fire.

'I have made up my mind, Sir,' he began, bending forward as soon as we were seated, and speaking in a tone but a little above a whisper, 'that you shall not have to ask me twice what troubles me. I took you for someone else yesterday evening. That troubles me.'

'That mistake?'

'No. That Someone else.'

'Who is it?'

'I don't know.'

'Like me?'

'I don't know. I never saw the face. The left arm is across the face, and the right arm is waved – violently waved. This way.'

COMMENTARY

As arranged, the story-teller returns the following night. The signalman begins to recount how he has seen a strange figure near the tunnel entrance.

to that effect: of that kind
sensation: imagined idea
Punctual to my appointment: On time for my meeting
took you: i.e. mistook you

I followed his action with my eyes, and it was the action of an arm gesticulating with the utmost passion and vehemence, 'For God's sake, clear the way!'

'One moonlight night,' said the man, 'I was sitting here when I heard a voice cry, "Halloa! Below there!" I started up, looked from that door, and saw this Someone else standing by the red light near the tunnel, waving as I just now showed you. The voice seemed hoarse with shouting, and it cried: "Look out! Look out!" I caught up my lamp, turned it on red, and ran towards the figure, calling, "What's wrong? What has happened? Where?" It stood just outside the blackness of the tunnel. I advanced so close upon it that I wondered at its keeping the sleeve across its eyes. I ran right up at it, and had my hand stretched out to pull the sleeve away, when it was gone.'

'Into the tunnel?' said I.

'No. I ran on into the tunnel, five hundred yards. I stopped, and held my lamp above my head, and saw the figures of the measured distance, and saw the wet stains stealing down the walls and trickling through the arch. I ran out again faster than I had run in (for I had a mortal abhorrence of the place upon me), and I looked all round the red light with my own red light, and I went up the iron ladder to the gallery atop of it, and I came down again, and ran back here. I telegraphed both ways. "An alarm has been given. Is anything wrong?" The answer came back, both ways, "All well."'

Resisting the slow touch of a frozen finger tracing out my spine, I showed him how this figure must be a deception of his sense of sight; and how that figure, originating in disease of the delicate nerves that minister to the functions of the eye, were known to have often troubled patients, some of whom had become conscious of the nature of their affliction, and had even proved it by experiments upon themselves. 'As to an imaginary cry,' said I, 'do but listen for a moment to the wind in this unnatural valley while we speak so low, and to the wild harp it makes of the telegraph wires.'

---

gesticulating with the utmost passion and vehemence: signalling frantically and with great urgency

figures of the measured distance: on the walls of the tunnel, its length is marked off in yards

mortal abhorrence: deadly terror and hatred

deception of his sense of sight: an optical illusion

originating in disease...of the eye: caused by a disease of the optic nerves

affliction: illness, problem

COMMENTARY

The figure shouted and gestured as if there had been an accident. When the signalman had almost reached it, the figure vanished. There was nothing wrong in the tunnel. The nearest stations up and down the line reported all well.

That was all very well, he returned, after we had sat listening for a while, and he ought to know something of the wind and the wires – he who so often passed long winter nights there, alone and watching. But he would beg to remark that he had not finished.

I asked his pardon, and he slowly added these words, touching my arm:

'Within six hours after the Appearance, the memorable accident on this Line happened, and within ten hours the dead and wounded were brought along through the tunnel over the spot where the figure had stood.'

A disagreeable shudder crept over me, but I did my best against it. It was not to be denied, I rejoined, that this was a remarkable coincidence, calculated deeply to impress his mind. But it was unquestionable that remarkable coincidences did continually occur, and they must be taken into account in dealing with such a subject. Though to be sure I must admit, I added (for I thought I saw that he was going to bring the objection to bear upon me), men of common sense did not allow much for coincidences in making the ordinary calculations of life.

He again begged to remark that he had not finished.

I again begged his pardon for being betrayed into interruptions.

'This,' he said, laying his hand upon my arm, and glancing over his shoulder with hollow eyes, 'was just a year ago. Six or seven months passed, and I had recovered from the surprise and shock, when one morning, as the day was breaking, I, standing at the door, looked towards the red light, and saw the spectre again.' He stopped, with a fixed a look at me.

'Did it cry out?'

'No. It was silent.'

'Did it wave its arm?'

'No. It leaned against the shaft of the light, with both hands before the face. Like this.'

Once more I followed his action with my eyes. It was an action of mourning. I have seen such an attitude in stone figures on tombs.

'Did you go up to it?'

COMMENTARY

The signalman has more to tell. Only hours after he saw the 'spectre', a dreadful accident happened in the tunnel. Coincidence, suggests the storyteller.

Six months later, the same figure reappeared at the tunnel entrance.

returned: replied

calculated deeply to impress his mind: bound to leave a strong impression on his memory

attitude: i.e. with both hands held in front of the face

'I came in and sat down, partly to collect my thoughts, partly because it had turned me faint. When I went to the door again, daylight was above me, and the ghost was gone.'

'But nothing followed? Nothing came of this?'

He touched me on the arm with his forefinger twice or thrice, giving a ghastly nod each time:

'That very day, as a train came out of the tunnel, I noticed, at a carriage window on my side, what looked like a confusion of hands and heads, and something waved. I saw it just in time to signal to the driver, Stop! He shut off, and put his brake on, but the train drifted past here a hundred and fifty yards or more. I ran after it, and, as I went along, heard terrible screams and cries. A beautiful young lady had died instantaneously in one of the compartments, and was brought in here, and laid down on this floor between us.'

Involuntarily I pushed my chair back, as I looked from the boards at which he pointed to himself.

'True, Sir. True. Precisely as it happened, so I tell it you.'

I could think of nothing to say, to any purpose, and my mouth was very dry. The wind and the wires took up the story with a long lamenting wail.

He resumed. 'Now Sir, mark this, and judge how my mind is troubled. The spectre came back a week ago. Ever since, it has been there, now and again, by fits and starts.

'At the light?'

'At the Danger-light.'

'What does it seem to do?'

He repeated, if possible with increased passion and vehemence, that former gesticulation of 'For God's sake, clear the way!'

Then he went on. 'I have no peace or rest for it. It calls to me – for many minutes together, in an agonised manner, "Below there! Look out! Look out!" It stands waving to me. It rings my little bell – '

I caught at that. 'Did it ring your bell yesterday evening when I was here, and you went to the door?'

instantaneously: suddenly
Involuntarily: without intending to
lamenting: mournful
mark this: listen carefully
passion and vehemence: urgency and emphasis
agonised: very distressed
caught at that: took him up on that remark

COMMENTARY
This time, the ghostly figure was silent – it simply looked to be in mourning. The same day, a woman died on a train as it passed through the tunnel.

During the last week, the spectre has appeared several times to the signalman in its usual place.

'Twice.'

'Why, see,' I said, 'how your imagination misleads you. My eyes were on the bell, and my ears were open to the bell, and if I am a living man, it did NOT ring at those times. No, nor at any other time, except when it was rung in the natural course of physical things by the station communicating with you.'

He shook his head. 'I have never made a mistake as to that yet, Sir. I have never confused the spectre's ring with the man's. The ghost's ring is a strange vibration in the bell that it derives from nothing else, and I have not asserted that the bell stirs to the eye. I don't wonder that you failed to hear it. But *I* heard it.'

'And did the spectre seem to be there, when you looked out?'

'It WAS there.'

'Both times?'

He repeated firmly, 'Both times.'

'Will you come to the door with me, and look for it now?'

He bit his under lip as though he were somewhat unwilling, but arose. I opened the door, and stood on the step, while he stood in the doorway. There was the Danger-light. There was the dismal mouth of the tunnel. There were the high, wet stone walls of the cutting. There were the stars above them.

'Do you see it?' I asked him, taking particular note of his face.

His eyes were prominent and strained, but not very much more so, perhaps, that my own had been when I had directed them earnestly towards the same spot.

'No,' he answered. 'It is not there.'

'Agreed,' said I.

We went in again, shut the door, and resumed our seats. I was thinking how best to improve this advantage, if it might be called one, when he took up the conversation in such a matter-of-course way, so assuming that there could be no serious question of fact between us, that I felt myself in the weakest of positions.

'By this time you will fully understand, Sir,' he said, 'that what troubles me so dreadfully is the question, What does the spectre mean?'

COMMENTARY

In the box, the signalman's bell often rings, but only he can hear it. When the story-teller was with him the night before, this happened twice – and twice the signalman saw the spectre standing by the Danger-light at the mouth of the tunnel.

asserted: stated
directed them earnestly: looked intently
improve this advantage: make the most of the 'proof'

I was not sure, I told him, that I did fully understand.

'What is its warning against?' he said, ruminating, with his eyes on the fire, and only by times turning them on me. 'What is the danger? Where is the danger? There is danger overhanging somewhere on the Line. Some dreadful calamity will happen. It is not to be doubted this third time, after what has gone before. But surely this is a cruel haunting of *me*. What can *I* do?'

He pulled out his handkerchief, and wiped the drops from his heated forehead.

'If I telegraph Danger, on either side of me, or on both, I can give no reason for it,' he went on, wiping the palms of his hands. 'I should get into trouble, and do no good. They would think I was mad. This is the way it would work – Message: "Danger! Take Care!" Answer: "What danger? Where?" Message: "Don't know. But, for God's sake, take care!" They would displace me. What else could they do?'

His pain of mind was most pitiable to see. It was the mental torture of a conscientious man, oppressed beyond endurance by an unintelligible responsibility involving life.

'When it first stood under the Danger-light,' he went on, putting his dark hair back from his head, and drawing his hands outward and across his temples in an extremity of feverish distress, 'why not tell me where that accident was to happen – if it might happen? Why not tell me how it could be averted – if it could be averted? When on its second coming it hid its face, why not tell me instead, "She is going to die. Let them keep her at home"? If it came, on those two occasions, only to show me that its warnings were true, and so prepare me for the third, why not warn me plainly now? And I, Lord help me! A mere poor signalman on this solitary station! Why not go to somebody with credit to be believed and power to act?'

When I saw him in this state, I saw that for the poor man's sake, as well as for the public safety, what I had to do for the time was to compose his mind. Therefore, setting aside all question of reality or unreality between us, I represented to him that whoever thoroughly discharged his duty must do well,

ruminating: thinking deeply

displace me: give me the sack

conscientious man...involving life: an honest man weighed down by his responsibilities and not knowing how to act for the best

averted: prevented

solitary station: lonely outpost

with credit to be believed: with the authority to be taken seriously

compose: calm

represented: suggested

COMMENTARY

The story-teller tries 'proving' that the spectre is not in sight now. It makes no difference to the signalman; he is near breaking-point. At a loss to know why he is being haunted, he thinks he will lose his job if he tells his fears to his employers. They will think him mad.

and that at least it was his comfort that he understood his duty, though he did not understand these confounding Appearances. In this effort I succeeded far better than in the attempt to reason him out of his conviction. He became calm; the occupations incidental to his post as the night advanced began to make larger demands on his attention; and I left him at two in the morning. I had offered to stay through the night, but he would not hear of it.

That I more than once looked back at the red light as I ascended the pathway, that I did not like the red light, and that I should have slept but poorly if my bed had been under it, I see no reason to conceal. Nor did I like the two sequences of the accident and the dead girl. I see no reason to conceal that either.

But what ran most in my thoughts was the consideration how I ought to act, having become the recipient of this disclosure? I had proved the man to be intelligent, vigilant, painstaking, and exact; but how long might he remain so, in his state of mind? Though in a subordinate position, still he held a most important trust, and would I (for instance) like to stake my own life on the chances of his continuing to execute it with precision?

Unable to overcome a feeling that there would be something treacherous in my communicating what he had told me to his superiors in the Company, without first being plain with himself and proposing a middle course to him, I ultimately resolved to offer to accompany him (otherwise keeping his secret for the present) to the wisest medical practitioner we could hear of in those parts, and to take his opinion. A change in his time of duty would come round next night, he had apprised me, and he would be off an hour or two after sunrise, and on again soon after sunset. I had appointed to return accordingly.

Next evening was a lovely evening, and I walked out early to enjoy it. The sun was not yet quite down when I traversed the field-path near the top of the deep cutting. I would extend my walk for an hour, I said to myself, half an hour on and half an hour back, and it would then be time to go to my signalman's box.

confounding: bewildering
the recipient of this disclosure: the person who has heard his story
subordinate position: an employee
execute it with precision: carry it out carefully and safely
medical practitioner: doctor
apprised: informed
traversed: walked across

Before pursuing my stroll, I stepped to the brink, and mechanically looked down, from the point from which I had first seen him. I cannot describe the thrill that seized me, when, close at the mouth of the tunnel, I saw the appearance of a man, with his left sleeve across his eyes, passionately waving his right arm.

The nameless horror that oppressed me passed in a moment, for in a moment I saw this appearance of a man was a man indeed, and that there was a little group of other men, standing at a short distance, to whom he seemed to be rehearsing the gesture he made. The Danger-light was not yet lighted. Against its shaft, a little low hut, entirely new to me, had been made of some wooden supports and tarpaulin. It looked no bigger than a bed.

With an irresistible sense that something was wrong – with a flashing self-reproachful fear that fatal mischief had come of my leaving the man there, and causing no one to be sent to overlook or correct what he did – I descended the notched path with all the speed I could make.

'What is the matter?' I asked the men.

'Signalman killed this morning, Sir.'

'Not the man belonging to that box?'

'Yes, Sir.'

'Not the man I know?'

'You will recognise him, Sir, if you knew him,' said the man who spoke for the others, solemnly uncovering his own head, and raising an end of the tarpaulin, 'for his face is quite composed.'

'Oh, how did this happen, how did this happen?' I asked, turning from one to another as the hut closed in again.

'He was cut down by an engine, Sir. No man in England knew his work better. But somehow he was not clear of the outer rail. It was just at broad day. He had struck the light, and had the lamp in his hand. As the engine came out of the tunnel his back was towards her, and she cut him down. That man drove her, and was showing how it happened. Show the gentleman, Tom.'

---

thrill: feeling of terror
self-reproachful: self-blaming
composed: peaceful-looking
struck: lit

COMMENTARY
The following evening the story-teller sets out again for the signal-box. A figure is standing at the mouth of the tunnel, just like the spectre, frantically waving. A small group of men is standing near by, and a small hut has been built beneath the Danger-light.

The man, who wore a rough dark dress, stepped back to his former place at the mouth of the tunnel.

'Coming round the curve in the tunnel, Sir,' he said, 'I saw him at the end, like as if I saw him down a perspective-glass. There was no time to check speed, and I knew him to be very careful. As he didn't seem to take heed of the whistle, I shut it off when we were running down upon him, and called to him as loud as I could call.'

'What did you say?'

'I said, "Below there! Look out! Look out! For God's sake, clear the way!"'

I started.

'Ah! it was a dreadful time, Sir. I never left off calling to him. I put this arm before my eyes not to see, and I waved this arm to the last; but it was no use.'

Without prolonging the narrative to dwell on any one of its curious circumstances more than on any other, I may, in closing it, point out the coincidence that the warning of the Engine-driver included not only the words which the unfortunate Signalman had repeated to me as haunting him, but also the words which I myself – not he – had attached, and that only in my own mind, to the gesticulation he had imitated.

PAUSE FOR PLAYBACK:
Now look at the playback questions on page 24.

COMMENTARY
The signalman is dead. Standing at the tunnel entrance after lighting the Danger-light, he was struck by an engine and killed. The driver blew his whistle, called out and waved to him – but the signalman seemed not to notice these warnings.

dress: uniform
perspective-glass: telescope
prolonging the narrative: adding further to the story
attached: added
gesticulation: i.e. one arm in front of his eyes and the other arm waving

Study guide

PLAYBACK QUESTIONS

PAGES 9 TO 14:

➤ At first, the signalman neither hears nor sees the story-teller. Why not?
➤ Where does the signalman think he has seen the story-teller before?
➤ Why do you think the author makes a point of letting us know that the signalman is well-educated (see page 12)?
➤ 'but I am troubled, Sir, I am troubled'. From what you have read so far, what do you think it might be that 'troubles' the signalman?

Now return to reading the story on page 14

PAGES 15 TO 23:

➤ What does the ghost (or 'spectre') do when it appears to the signalman by the side of his red light? What happens shortly afterwards?
➤ Why is the signalman sure that it is the ghost rather than a human being which makes his electric bell ring?
➤ 'When on its second coming it hid its face, why not tell me instead, "She is going to die. Let them keep her at home"?' (page 20). In the light of the whole story, what is *your* answer to the signalman's question?
➤ The driver of the train that kills the signalman shouts out the same words of warning as the ghost. What do you make of this?

REVIEWING THE WHOLE STORY: SUGGESTED ACTIVITIES

1 Post mortem

A week after the signalman dies, a post-mortem enquiry is held into the cause of his death. In this activity, you are asked to provide various items of evidence to be used at the post mortem.

a **As a class**, discuss with your teacher exactly what a post mortem is. Why is it necessary? Who sets it up? What kinds of evidence have to be presented at it? What is the post-mortem report used for?

b **By yourself**, imagine you are the driver of the train which ran down the signalman. Re-read the last two pages of the story. Then, in your own words and in Standard English, write an accident report setting out as clearly as possible your version of what happened.

c **With a partner**, put yourself in the place of two of the members of the signalman's family: his wife, and his eldest child (who lives at home and who is in his/her late twenties). Your evidence will be about the signalman's behaviour during the last year.

Imagine what changes you are likely to have noticed in him. Have you been worried about him? How much has he told you about the events that have 'troubled' him? Has he shown signs of having other problems? Working together, write a joint statement that will be read out on your behalf at the post mortem.

d **In a group**, discuss the evidence which will be presented by the 'key witness' at the post mortem: the story-teller. Ask yourselves:

- how much of what he knows will he be prepared to reveal?

- will he be anxious about his story – or parts of it – being believed?

- will he be afraid that he could, to some extent, be held responsible for the signalman's death?

- what explanation will he decide to put forward of why the signalman died?

In your discussion, bear in mind what the story shows about the story-teller's character. His evidence should be consistent with this.

e Finally, stay **in your group** and role-play the story-teller's appearance at the post mortem where he is called to give evidence. Decide who will take his part. Other group members, in the role of investigators, can then question him.

2 Powers of darkness

Many readers find *The Signalman* such a gripping story because it can be understood in more than one way. This activity asks you to decide for yourself what evidence there is for seeing it as a story about the forces of evil as they affect human life.

a   **As a class**, discuss the central question Dickens raises about the signalman: *why* is he being haunted – and by whom? Consider in turn the following possibilities:

- the ghost is warning him about accidents that are about to happen so that he can take steps to prevent them.

- the ghost is someone who died in a railway accident in the past. It appears when another accident is due, but is powerless to tell the signalman exactly when and where it will happen.

- the ghost has the power to bring about people's deaths. It deliberately torments the signalman to the point of causing him a mental breakdown, and, at the end of the story, lures him to his *own* death.

What evidence can you find from the text to support these three different 'versions'. Which one do *you* think is the most convincing?

In the course of your discussion, have you come up with any other explanations of why the signalman is being haunted?

b   **In a group**, look further into the *third* version presented above, which suggests that the ghost is 'evil' and deliberately brings about death and destruction. Examine the evidence for this by drawing and filling out a 'haunting cycle', like this:

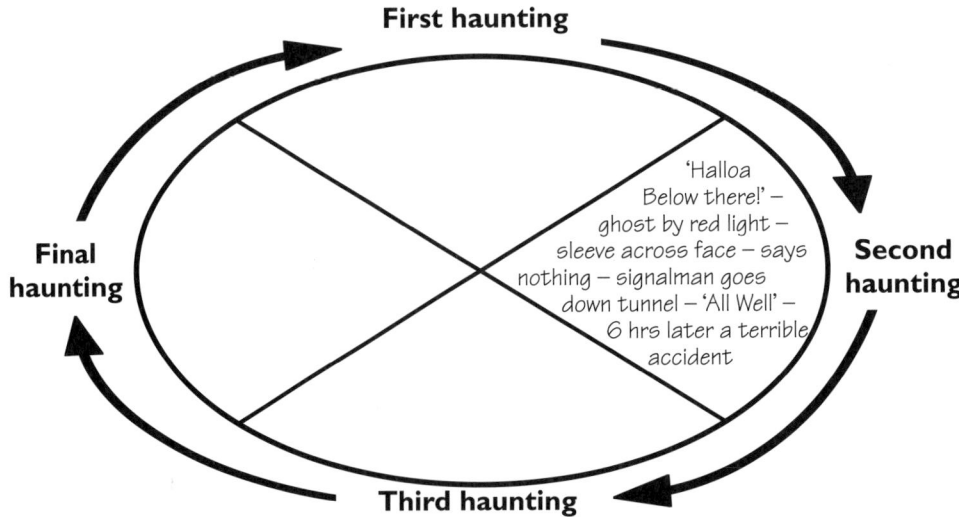

(The order of the four hauntings follows the order in which the story-teller presents them. Thus the first haunting is the one described on the opening page, and the final haunting is the one that leads to the signalman's death.)

Talk about what your completed cycles show. Ask yourselves:

- what pattern do the hauntings follow?

- after each haunting, what do you notice about the signalman's state of mind?

- what do you make of the fact that, when the signalman first saw the story-teller, he thought *he* was the ghost?

c   **As a class**, re-read the last part of the story. Begin from 'He was cut down by an engine, Sir' (page 22) and go on to the end.

Consider whether there are any grounds for thinking that the signalman either (i) took his own life, or (ii) at least made no attempt to avoid being 'cut down' by the engine.

d   **By yourself**, use the work you have done during this activity to write your own version of who – or what – the ghost is and why it haunts the signalman. Quote from the text to back up the ideas you put forward.

3 | Drawing out the story

The illustrations on the front of this volume and on page 8 show how a professional artist 'sees' the story. Do they match up with your impressions of *The Signalman*?

a   **With a partner**, look closely at each illustration in turn. Notice its details: the more you look, the more you will find. Then give both of them a suitable caption, which can be *either* a short quotation from the story itself *or* something you make up between you.

b   **By yourself**, write a brief commentary on each illustration. It should say:

- which part of the story is being pictured – and how you know.

- what kind of *atmosphere* each illustration creates – and whether it is suited to the story as a whole.

- whether you feel the artist has made good choices of what to illustrate – or whether he should have made different ones.

4 'This great dungeon'

In *The Signalman*, everything happens in the same place or setting. This activity asks you to consider how Dickens uses his chosen setting to increase the story's impact on the reader.

a   **By yourself**, re-read the paragraph on pages 10 to 11 beginning 'I resumed my downward way' and ending 'as if I had left the natural world'. Pick out at least *six* words from this extract which describe the atmosphere of the railway cutting. Jot them down on a sheet of paper, leaving a sizeable space between and around each.

b   **With a partner**, compare the words you have chosen. Are they the same, or similar?

   Ask yourselves:

   ● what impressions of the railway cutting do your words give – and what do these impressions have in common?

   ● does the story-teller react to where he is with any senses other than his sense of sight?

   ● if this paragraph came near the beginning of *another* story, what sort of things would you expect to happen in it?

c   **As a class**, use your word-lists to examine the atmosphere in the rest of the story. With your teacher, look at particular descriptions later on in the story. As you find words and phrases *from the text* that match up with those you have already listed, write them into the spaces you left. Decide on the most suitable place to put them, and include page references for each.

d   **In a group** or **as a class**, discuss the importance of the following facts to the story as a whole:

   ● until the signalman dies, everything happens in the darkness of night.

   ● the signalman is repeatedly 'drawn' to the tunnel, about which he says 'I had a mortal abhorrence [i.e. dislike and terror] of the place'.

   ● several times the story-teller refers to the railway cutting as 'unnatural' and 'unhealthy'.

e   **By yourself**, use the work you have done during this activity to write on the following title:

   'Dickens's descriptions of the railway cutting create a strong atmosphere which is well suited to the plot of *The Signalman*.'
   Do you agree?

   Use your notes to find quotations that will support the points you make.

5 | 'Nameless horror'

The Signalman has the reputation of being one of the most effective stories of the supernatural ever written. The purpose of this activity is for you to decide how good a story *you* consider it to be.

a **As a class** or **in a group**, discuss what 'ingredients' a really memorable ghost story ought to have in order to hold the reader's interest. Draw on your reading of other such stories, and your experience of watching videos and films, to illustrate your ideas.

b Each make a list of the ingredients you agree about. Try to list between six and ten. Include not only *what* the story contains but also aspects of *the way in which it is written*.

c **By yourself**, make a 'circle-gram' to show what ingredients *you* think are of most importance. These may or may not reflect your class/group discussion. Set it out like this:

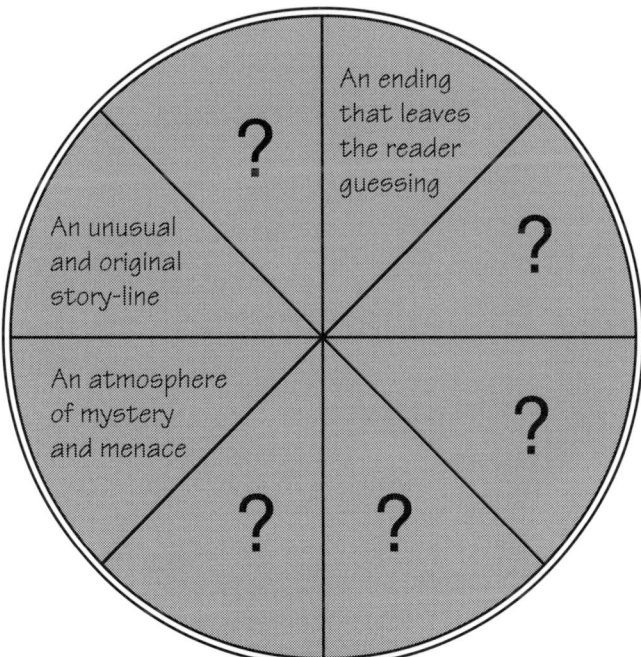

d Using your circle-gram, take part in a **class discussion** about the supernatural or ghostly ingredients in *The Signalman* – and how effective they are.

e **By yourself**, write an honest assessment of *The Signalman* as a story of the supernatural. Give clear reasons for the points you make and support them with quotations from the text.

CONFESSION FOUND IN A PRISON

Look out for...

- why the story-teller, or 'narrator', has committed the crime for which he is in prison.
- the narrator's feelings towards his brother, his sister-in-law, and his nephew.

I held a lieutenant's commission in His Majesty's Army, and served abroad in the campaigns of 1677 and 1678. The treaty of Nimegen being concluded, I returned home, and retiring from the service withdrew to a small estate lying a few miles east of London, which I had recently acquired in right of my wife.

This is the last night I have to live, and I will set down the naked truth without disguise. I was never a brave man, and had always been from my childhood of a secret, sullen and distrustful nature. I speak of myself as if I had passed from the world, for while I write this my grave is digging and my name is written in the black book of death.

Soon after my return to England, my only brother was seized with mortal illness. This circumstance gave me slight or no pain, for since we had been men we associated but very little together. He was open-hearted and generous, handsomer than I, more accomplished, and generally beloved. Those who sought my acquaintance abroad or at home because they were friends of his, seldom attached themselves to me long, and would usually say in our first conversation that they were surprised to find two brothers so unlike in their manners and appearance. It was my habit to lead them on to this avowal, for I

COMMENTARY

The narrator is in a condemned cell on the night before his execution. He is writing his confession to the world. Soon after he left the Army, he says, his brother fell ill with a fatal disease – an event which caused him no real sadness or regret.

commission: rank, post
in right of my wife: through a legacy left to my wife
mortal: fatal
but: only
sought my acquaintance: tried to make friends with me
long: for a long time
avowal: observation

knew what comparisons they must draw between us, and having a rankling envy in my heart, I sought to justify it to myself.

We had married two sisters. This additional tie between us, as it may appear to some, only estranged us the more. His wife knew me well. I never struggled with any secret jealousy or gall when she was present but that woman knew it as well as I did. I never raised my eyes at such times but I found hers fixed upon me; I never bent them on the ground or looked another way, but I felt that she overlooked me always. It was an inexpressible relief to me when we quarrelled, and a greater relief still when I heard abroad that she was dead. It seems to me now as if some strange and terrible foreshadowing of what has happened since, must have hung over us then. I was afraid of her, she haunted me; her fixed and steady look comes back upon me now like the memory of a dark dream and makes my blood run cold.

She died shortly after giving birth to a child – a boy. When my brother knew that all hope of his own recovery was past, he called my wife to his bed-side and confided this orphan, a child of four years old, to her protection. He bequeathed to him all the property he had, and willed that in case of the child's death, it should pass to my wife as the only acknowledgement he could make for her care and love. He exchanged a few brotherly words with me, deploring our long separation, and being exhausted, fell into a slumber from which he never awoke.

We had no children; and as there had been a strong affection between the sisters, and my wife had almost supplied the place of a mother to this boy, she loved him as if he had been her own. The child was ardently attached to her; but he was his mother's image in face and spirit and always mistrusted me.

I can scarcely fix the date when the feeling first came upon me, but I soon began to be uneasy when this child was by. I never roused myself from some moody train of thought but I marked him looking at me: not with mere childish wonder, but with something of the purpose and meaning that I had so often noted in his mother. It was no effort of my fancy, founded on close resemblance of feature and expression. I never could look the boy down. He

---

rankling envy: painful jealousy
estranged us the more: drove us still
   further apart
gall: bitterness
foreshadowing: premonition
confided: entrusted
bequeathed: left in his will
ardently: lovingly, passionately
by: i.e. near to me
marked: noticed
no effort of my fancy: not the work of my
   imagination

COMMENTARY
The narrator's sister-in-law died soon after the birth of her son. When the boy was 4 years old, his father died too, leaving the child to be brought up by the narrator's wife. The boy will inherit everything his parents had. Although very young, he shares his dead mother's dislike and distrust of his uncle.

feared me, but seemed by some instinct to despise me while he did so; and even when he drew back beneath my gaze – as he would when we were alone, to get nearer to the door – he would keep his bright eyes upon me still.

Perhaps I hide the truth from myself, but I do not think that when this began, I meditated to do him any wrong. I may have thought how serviceable his inheritance would be to us, and may have wished him dead, but I believe I had no thought of compassing his death. Neither did the idea come upon me at once, but by slow degrees, presenting itself at first in dim shapes, at a very great distance, as men may think of an earthquake or the last day – then drawing nearer and nearer and losing something of its horror and improbability – then coming to be part and parcel, nay nearly the whole sum and substance of my daily thoughts and resolving itself into a question of means and safety; not of doing or abstaining from the deed.

While this was going on within me, I never could bear that the child should see me looking at him, and yet I was under a fascination which made it a kind of business with me to contemplate his slight and fragile figure and think how easily it might be done. Sometimes I would steal upstairs and watch him as he slept, but usually I hovered in the garden near the window of the room in which he learned his little tasks, and there as he sat upon a low seat with my wife, I would peer at him for hours together from behind a tree: starting like the guilty wretch I was at every rustling of a leaf, and still gliding back to look and start again.

Hard by our cottage, but quite out of sight, and (if there were any wind astir) of hearing too, was a deep sheet of water. I spent days in shaping with my pocket-knife a rough model of a boat, which I finished at last and dropped in the child's way. Then I withdrew to a secret place which he must pass if he stole away alone to swim this bauble, and lurked there for his coming. He came neither that day nor the next, though I waited from noon till nightfall. I was sure that I had him in my net for I had heard him prattling of the toy, and knew that in his infant pleasure he kept it by his side in bed. I felt no weariness or fatigue, but waited patiently, and on the third day he passed me,

COMMENTARY
The narrator believes the boy is continually watching him with the same contempt that his mother had. Slowly, the idea of murdering his nephew grows in the narrator's mind. He begins planning how to do it.

meditated: planned, intended
serviceable: useful, beneficial
compassing: bringing about
abstaining: holding back
Hard by: A short distance away from
bauble: i.e. the toy boat
prattling: chattering childishly

running joyously along, with his silken hair streaming in the wind and he singing – God have mercy upon me! – singing a merry ballad – who could hardly lisp the words.

I stole down after him, creeping under certain shrubs which grow in that place, and none but devils know with what terror I, a full-grown man, tracked the footsteps of that baby as he approached the water's brink. I was close upon him, had sunk upon my knee and raised my hand to thrust him in, when he saw my shadow in the stream and turned round.

His mother's ghost was looking from his eyes. The sun burst forth from behind a cloud: it shone in the bright sky, the glistening earth, the clear water, the sparkling drops of rain upon the leaves. There were eyes in everything. The whole great universe of light was there to see the murder done. I know not what he said; he came of bold and manly blood, and child as he was, he did not crouch or fawn upon me. I heard him cry that he would try to love me – not that he did – and then I saw him running back towards the house. The next I saw was my own sword naked in my hand and he lying at my feet stark dead – dabbled here and there with blood but otherwise no different from what I had seen him in his sleep – in the same attitude too, with his cheek resting upon his little hand.

PAUSE FOR PLAYBACK:
Now look at the playback questions on page 39 before going on with your reading.

Look out for...
- **how the narrator tries to conceal his crime.**
- **the unexpected way in which it finally comes to light.**
- **the narrator's feelings as he awaits his execution.**

came of: descended from
fawn upon: plead with
attitude: position

COMMENTARY
The narrator waits by a nearby pool for the boy to come and sail his boat. When the boy turns round, his mother's ghost is staring through his eyes. On impulse, the narrator runs him through with his sword.

I took him in my arms and laid him – very gently now that he was dead – in a thicket. My wife was from home that day and would not return until the next. Our bedroom window, the only sleeping room on that side of the house, was but a few feet from the ground, and I resolved to descend from it at night and bury him in the garden. I had no thought that I had failed in my design, no thought that the water would be dragged and nothing found, that the money must now lie waste since I must encourage the idea that the child was lost or stolen. All my thoughts were bound up and knotted together, in the one absorbing necessity of hiding what I had done.

How I felt when they came to tell me that the child was missing, when I ordered scouts in all directions, when I grasped and trembled at everyone's approach, no tongue can tell or mind of man conceive. I buried him that night. When I parted the boughs and looked into the dark thicket, there was a glow-worm like the visible spirit of God upon the murdered child. I glanced down into his grave when I had placed him there and still it gleamed upon his breast: an eye of fire looking up to Heaven in supplication to the stars that watched me at my work.

I had to meet my wife, and break the news, and give her hope that the child would soon be found. All this I did – with some appearance, I suppose, of being sincere, for I was the object of no suspicion. This done, I sat at the bedroom window all day long and watched the spot where the dreadful secret lay.

It was a piece of ground which had been dug up to be newly turfed, and which I had chosen on that account as the traces of my spade were less likely to attract attention. The men who laid down the grass must have thought me mad. I called to them continually to expedite their work, ran out and worked beside them, trod down the turf with my feet, and hurried them with frantic eagerness. They had finished their task before night, and then I thought myself comparatively safe.

I slept – not as men do who wake refreshed and cheerful, but I did sleep, passing from vague and shadowy dreams of being hunted down, to visions of

COMMENTARY

The narrator hides the dead body in a patch of open ground concealed by thick trees and buries it later that night in the garden. To avoid suspicion, he pretends that the boy has gone missing. His story is believed.

resolved: made my mind up
design: plan
absorbing necessity: urgent need
scouts: searchers
conceive: imagine
in supplication: as if asking a blessing
expedite: speed up

the plot of grass, through which now a hand, and now a foot, and now the head itself was starting out. At this point I always woke and stole to the window to make sure that it was not really so. That done, I crept to bed again; and thus I spent the night in fits and starts, getting up and lying down full twenty times, and dreaming the same dream over and over again – which was far worse than lying awake, for every dream had a whole night's suffering of its own. Once I thought the child was alive and that I had never tried to kill him. To wake from that dream was the most dreadful agony of all.

The next day I sat at the window again, never once taking my eyes from the place, which, although it was covered by the grass, was as plain to me – its shape, its size, its depth, its jagged sides, and all – as if it had been open to the light of day. When a servant walked across it, I felt as if he must sink in; when he had passed I looked to see that his feet had not worn the edges. If a bird lighted there, I was in terror lest by some tremendous interposition it should be instrumental in the discovery; if a breath of air sighed across it, to me it whispered murder. There was not a sight nor sound – how ordinary, mean or unimportant so ever – but was fraught with fear. And in this state of ceaseless watching I spent three days.

On the fourth, there came to the gate one who had served with me abroad, accompanied by a brother officer of his whom I had never seen. I felt that I could not bear to be out of sight of the place. It was a summer evening and I bade my people take a table and a flask of wine into the garden.

Then I sat down *with my chair upon the grave*, and being assured that nobody could disturb it now, without my knowledge, tried to drink and talk.

They hoped that my wife was well – that she was not obliged to keep her chamber – that they had not frightened her away. What could I do but tell them with a faltering tongue about the child? The officer whom I did not know was a down-looking man and kept his eyes upon the ground while I was speaking. Even that terrified me! I could not divest myself of the idea that he saw something there which caused him to suspect the truth. I asked him hurriedly if he supposed that – and stopped. 'That the child had been

---

starting: rising
lest by some...the discovery: in case by some
    remote chance it led to the grave being
    found
mean: slight
fraught with: filled with
one: i.e. an Army officer
bade: ordered
obliged to keep her chamber: confined to
    bed by illness
down-looking: shy, nervous
divest: rid

COMMENTARY
Although he has covered up his crime, the narrator lives in fear of being found out. He suffers terrible nightmares and needs to keep a constant watch over the grave.

Two Army officers pay a visit. The narrator takes them into the garden for refreshment.

murdered?' said he, looking mildly at me. 'Oh no! what could a man gain by murdering a poor child?' *I* could have told him what a man gained by such a deed, no one better, but I held my peace and shivered with an ague.

Mistaking my emotion, they were endeavouring to cheer me with the hope that the boy would certainly be found – great cheer that was for me! – when we heard a low deep howl, and presently there sprung over the wall two great dogs, who, bounding into the garden, repeated the baying sound we had heard before.

'Blood-hounds!' cried my visitors.

What need to tell me that! I had never seen one of that kind in all my life, but I knew what they were and for what purpose they had come. I grasped the elbows of my chair, and neither spoke nor moved.

'They are of the genuine breed,' said the man whom I had known abroad, 'and being out of exercise have no doubt escaped from their keeper.'

Both he and his friend turned to look at the dogs, who with their noses to the ground moved restlessly about, running to and fro, and up and down, and across, and round in circles, careering about like wild things, and all this time taking no notice of us, but ever and again repeating the yell we had heard already, then dropping their noses to the ground again and tracking earnestly here and there. They now began to snuff the earth more eagerly than they had done yet, and although they were still very restless, no longer beat about in such wide circuits, but kept near to one spot, and constantly diminished the distance between themselves and me.

At last they came up close to the great chair on which I sat, and raising their frightful howl once more, tried to tear away the wooden rails that kept them from the ground beneath. I saw how I looked, in the faces of the two who were with me.

'They scent some prey!' said they, both together.

'They scent no prey!' cried I.

'In Heaven's name, move!' said the one I knew, very earnestly, 'or you will be torn to pieces.'

COMMENTARY

The narrator is careful to place his own chair over the boy's grave. Suddenly, two blood-hounds leap over the garden wall and start tracking down a scent. They sniff out the boy's body below ground.

ague: fever, cold sweat
endeavouring: attempting
of the genuine breed: true blood-hound stock, pedigrees
careering: bounding
diminished: narrowed down

'Let them tear me limb from limb, I'll never leave this place!' cried I. 'Are dogs to hurry men to shameful deaths? Hew them down, cut them in pieces.'

'There is some foul mystery here!' said the officer whom I did not know, drawing his sword. 'In King Charles's name, assist me to secure this man.'

They both set about me and forced me away, though I fought and bit and caught at them like a madman. After a struggle, they got me quietly between them, and then, my God! I saw the angry dogs tearing at the earth and throwing it up into the air like water.

What more have I to tell? That I fell upon my knees, and with chattering teeth confessed the truth, and prayed to be forgiven. That I have since denied, and now confess to it again. That I have been tried for the crime, found guilty, and sentenced. That I have not the courage to anticipate my doom, or to bear up manfully against it. That I have no compassion, no consolation, no hope, no friend. That my wife has happily lost for the time those faculties which would enable her to know my misery or hers. That I am alone in this stone dungeon with my evil spirit, and that I die tomorrow!

PAUSE FOR PLAYBACK:
Now look at the playback questions on page 39.

Hew: Chop
secure: arrest, take captive
anticipate: think ahead to
compassion: pity
those faculties: i.e. her senses

COMMENTARY
When the narrator will not move either his chair or himself, the Army officers guess what he is hiding. After a struggle, they arrest him. He is tried – and he now awaits execution.

Study guide

PLAYBACK QUESTIONS

PAGES 31 TO 34:

➤ What can you tell about the narrator's character from the way he behaves towards his brother and his sister-in-law?
➤ Why do you think the narrator decides to kill his young nephew? At exactly what point does he reach his decision?
➤ How does the author make you feel sorry for the small boy?
➤ What do you think the narrator will now do to avoid being found out?

Now return to reading the story on page 34

PAGES 35 TO 38:

➤ How much does the narrator suffer from regret – and how much from the fear of discovery?
➤ Do you think the author tries to make us feel any sympathy for the murderer? If so, how?
➤ 'I knew what they [the blood-hounds] were and for what purpose they had come' (page 37). What does this tell you about the narrator's state of mind near the end of the story?
➤ Do you think that *everything* the narrator writes in the last paragraph is true? Why, or why not?

REVIEWING THE WHOLE STORY: SUGGESTED ACTIVITIES

1 The cover up

The murder is found out at the end of the story. However, the narrator almost succeeds in covering up his crime. This activity asks you to (i) examine how he does so and (ii) explore the one thing he *cannot* cover up – his fear of discovery.

a   **By yourself**, re-read the part of the story running from 'How I felt when they came to tell me that the child was missing' (page 35) to 'Hew them down, cut them in pieces' (page 38). Make a mental note of everything the murderer does to conceal the truth from other people.

b   **With a partner**, make a 'box chart' showing the various ways in which the murderer tries to hide what he has done. Draw six boxes, like this:

HIDING THE TRUTH

1. Sends out a search-party to look for the boy.	2.	3.
4.	5.	6.

You should be able to find six points, one for each box. Note them down in your *own* words.

c   **As a class**, find examples of how the murderer lives in constant fear after he has committed the murder. Talk about how his fears *grow* as time passes, quoting from the text to back up what you say. Make your own notes in the course of this discussion.

d   **By yourself**, write an account of the second half of *Confession Found in a Prison* using the following title:

'Describe the murderer's attempts to conceal his crime. Do you agree that they are defeated by his fear of discovery rather than by guilt?'

2 | A question of motive

Some of the things the murderer says about why he killed the boy suggest that he had clear motives. Other things are less clear: for instance, at more than one point he implies that he was driven to commit the crime almost against his will.

This activity asks you to investigate everything the murderer reveals about his motives – and to decide how fully he himself understands them.

In a group, imagine that the murderer's confession is examined after his execution by a committee of inquiry. Their task is to present a detailed verbal report to the coroner's court about why a 4-year-old boy was brutally murdered. You are the committee.

a   Begin your investigation by looking for the most 'obvious' possible motives. Money? Revenge? Jealousy?

Whenever you find evidence in the confession to support these (and other) motives, each make your own notes: you will need them later.

b   Now look at the possibility of more 'hidden' motives. For example, ask yourselves the following questions:

● the victim was the son of the murderer's brother. What do we know about the brothers' relationship?

● 'He was his mother's image in face and spirit' (page 32). What were the murderer's feelings towards his sister-in-law?

● and so on.

Keep on making your own notes as you talk.

c   Finally, look at the possibility of 'psychological' motives. Is there any evidence that the murderer was not fully in control of his actions and the feelings behind them? For instance, what do we make of a statement like:

'I was under a fascination which made it a kind of business with me to contemplate his slight and fragile figure and think how easily it might be done' (page 33)?

d   When your investigation is complete, prepare to present your findings to the coroner. You must report verbally on *all* the evidence you have examined before putting forward your conclusion.

Divide up the task of reporting between you. You can either present it 'live' or onto audio tape.

Your teacher may wish to use this activity to assess your Speaking and Listening skills.

THE TRIAL FOR MURDER

Look out for...
- **the way in which the story-teller becomes linked with a brutal murder in London.**
- **how the story-teller is affected by supernatural forces beyond his control.**

I have always noticed a prevalent want of courage, even among persons of superior intelligence and culture, as to imparting their own psychological experiences when those have been of a strange sort. Almost all men are afraid that what they could relate in such wise would find no parallel or response in a listener's internal life, and might be suspected or laughed at. A truthful traveller, who should have seen some extraordinary creature in the likeness of a sea-serpent, would have no fear of mentioning it; but the same traveller, having had some singular presentiment, impulse, vagary of thought, or vision (so-called), dream or other remarkable mental impression, would hesitate considerably before he would own to it. To this reticence I attribute much of the obscurity in which such subjects are involved. We do not habitually communicate our experiences of these subjective things as we do our experiences of objective creation. The consequence is that the general stock of experience in this regard appears exceptional, and really is so, in respect of being miserably imperfect.

In what I am going to relate, I have no intention of setting up, opposing, or supporting, any theory whatever. I know the history of the Bookseller of

COMMENTARY

The story-teller says that most of us shy away from talking about our experiences of the supernatural. As a result, too little is known about them – either through ignorance, or through prejudice.

prevalent want of courage: a frequent nervousness
imparting: describing to others
relate in such wise: tell about such things
singular: strange
presentiment: premonition of the future
vagary: oddity

own to: admit
reticence: holding back
attribute: ascribe, put down
We do not...objective creation: We don't normally speak as freely about our mental experiences as we do about our physical ones

Berlin. I have studied the case of the wife of a late Astronomer Royal as
related by Sir David Brewster, and I have followed the minutest details of the
much more remarkable case of Spectral Illusion occurring within my private
circle of friends. It may be necessary to state as to this last, that the sufferer (a
lady) was in no degree, however distant, related to me. A mistaken assumption
on that head might suggest an explanation of a part of my own case – but
only a part – which would be wholly without foundation. It cannot be referred
to my inheritance of any developed peculiarity, nor had I ever before any at all
similar experience, nor have I ever had any at all similar experience since.

It does not signify how many years ago, or how few, a certain murder was
committed in England, which attracted great attention. We hear more than
enough of murderers as they rise in succession to their atrocious eminence,
and I would bury the memory of this particular brute, if I could, as his body
was buried in Newgate Jail. I purposely abstain from giving any direct clue to
the criminal's individuality.

When the murder was first discovered, no suspicion fell – or I ought rather
to say, for I cannot be too precise in my facts, it was nowhere publicly hinted
that any suspicion fell – on the man who was afterwards brought to trial. As
no reference was at that time made to him in the newspapers, it is obviously
impossible that any description of him can at that time have been given in the
newspaper. It is essential that this fact be remembered.

Unfolding at breakfast my morning paper, containing the account of that
first discovery, I found it to be deeply interesting, and I read it with close
attention. I read it twice, if not three times. The discovery had been made in a
bedroom, and, when I laid down the paper, I was aware of a flash – rush – flow
– I do not know what to call it – no word I can find is satisfactorily descriptive
– in which I seemed to see that bedroom passing through my room, like a
picture impossibly painted on a running river. Though almost instantaneous
in its passing, it was perfectly clear; so clear that I distinctly, and with a sense
of relief, observed the absence of the dead body from the bed.

It was no romantic place that I had this curious sensation, but in chambers

---

Bookseller of Berlin; wife of a late
Astronomer Royal; Spectral Illusion: well-
   known nineteenth-century 'true' ghost
   stories
this last: the last-mentioned story
on that head: concerning that
signify: matter, make any difference
eminence: ill-fame, notoriety
abstain from: avoid
individuality: name
discovery: i.e. of the victim's body
instantaneous: like a flash
chambers: a set of furnished rooms

COMMENTARY
The story-teller has had a strange
psychic experience himself. It began
when he read a newspaper account of
a murder. The corpse was found in a
bedroom. As he read about this,
something remarkable occurred in his
mind.

in Piccadilly, very near to the corner of St James's Street. It was entirely new to me. I was in my easy-chair at the moment, and the sensation was accompanied with a peculiar shiver which started the chair from its position. (But it is to be noted that the chair ran easily on castors.) I went to one of the windows (there are two in the room, and the room is on the second floor) to refresh my eyes with the moving objects down in Piccadilly. It was a bright autumn morning, and the street was sparkling and cheerful. The wind was high. As I looked out, it brought down from the Park a quantity of fallen leaves, which a gust took, and whirled into a spiral pillar. As the pillar fell and the leaves dispersed, I saw two men on the opposite side of the way, going from West to East. They were one behind the other. The foremost man often looked back over his shoulder. The second man followed him, at a distance of some thirty paces, with his right hand menacingly raised. First, the singularity and steadiness of this threatening gesture in so public a thoroughfare attracted my attention; and next, the more remarkable circumstance that nobody heeded it. Both men threaded their way among the other passengers with a smoothness hardly consistent even with the action of walking on a pavement; and no single creature, that I could see, gave them place, touched them, or looked after them. In passing before my windows, they both stared up at me. I saw their two faces very distinctly, and I knew that I could recognise them anywhere. Not that I consciously noticed anything very remarkable in either face, except that the man who went first had an unusually lowering appearance, and that the face of the man who followed him was the colour of impure wax.

I am a bachelor, and my valet and his wife constitute my whole establishment. My occupation is in a certain Branch Bank, and I wish that my duties as head of a Department were as light as they are popularly supposed to be. They kept me in town that autumn, when I stood in need of change. I was not ill, but I was not well. My reader is to make the most that can be reasonably made of my feeling jaded, having a depressing sense upon me of a monotonous life, and being 'slightly dyspeptic'. I am assured by my renowned doctor that my real state of health at that time justifies no stronger

---

COMMENTARY
The story-teller clearly 'saw' the room where the murder was committed. Looking out of his window, his gaze then fell on two men walking down the street. One of them seemed about to strike the other. The pedestrians were unaware of them. Both men, though, stared up at the story-teller's window.

---

started: jerked, jolted
menacingly: in a violent manner
singularity: highly uncommon sight
heeded it: paid it any attention
gave them place: moved out of the way to
   let them pass
lowering: scowling, sullen

valet: manservant
constitute: make up, comprise
establishment: household
Bank: the story-teller will from now on
   be referred to as 'the banker'
jaded: worn out
dyspeptic: suffering from indigestion

description, and I quote his own from his written answer to my request for it.

As the circumstances of the murder, gradually unravelling, took stronger and stronger possession of the public mind, I kept them away from mine by knowing as little about them as was possible in the midst of the universal excitement. But I knew that a verdict of Wilful Murder had been found against the suspected murderer, and that he had been committed to Newgate for trial. I also knew that his trial had been postponed over one Session of the Central Criminal Court, on the ground of general prejudice and want of time for the preparation of the defence. I may further have known, but I believe I did not, when, or about when, the Sessions to which his trial stood postponed would come on.

My sitting-room, bedroom, and dressing-room, are all on one floor. With the last there is no communication but through the bedroom. True, there is a door in it, once communicating with the staircase; but a part of the fitting of my bath has been – and had then been for some years – fixed across it. At the same period, and as a part of the same arrangement, the door had been nailed up and canvased over.

I was standing in my bedroom late one night, giving some directions to my servant before he went to bed. My face was towards the only available door of communication with the dressing-room, and it was closed. My servant's back was towards that door. While I was speaking to him I saw it open, and a man look in, who very earnestly and mysteriously beckoned to me. That man was the man who had gone second of the two along Piccadilly, and whose face was the colour of impure wax.

The figure, having beckoned, drew back, and closed the door. With no longer pause than was made by my crossing the bedroom, I opened the dressing-room door, and looked in. I had a lighted candle already in my hand. I felt no inward expectation of seeing the figure in the dressing-room, and I did not see it there.

Conscious that my servant stood amazed, I turned round to him, and said: 'Derrick, could you believe that in my cool senses I fancied I saw a...' As I

general prejudice: a strong feeling against him which made a fair trial impossible
earnestly: forcefully, urgently
my cool senses: my right mind

COMMENTARY
The banker (see glossary on page 45) takes little interest in the trial for murder. He only knows it has been postponed.

One night, the banker 'sees' another strange image: the man in the street who appeared violent looks through the door of his bedroom and beckons him.

there laid my hand upon his breast, with a sudden start he trembled violently, and said: 'O Lord, yes, Sir! A dead man beckoning!'

Now I do not believe that this John Derrick, my trusty and attached servant for more than twenty years, had any impression whatever of having seen any such figure, until I touched him. The change in him was so startling, when I touched him, that I fully believe he derived his impression in some occult manner from me at that instant.

I bade John Derrick bring some brandy, and I gave him a dram, and was glad to take one myself. Of what had preceded that night's phenomenon, I told him not a single word. Reflecting on it, I was absolutely certain that I had never seen that face before, except on the one occasion in Piccadilly. Comparing its expression when beckoning at the door with its expression when it had stared up at me as I stood at my window, I came to the conclusion that on the first occasion it had sought to fasten itself upon my memory, and that on the second it had made sure of being immediately remembered.

I was not very comfortable that night, though I felt a certainty, difficult to explain, that the figure would not return. At daylight I fell into a heavy sleep, from which I was awakened by John Derrick's coming to my bedside with a paper in his hand.

This paper, it appeared, had been the subject of an altercation at the door between its bearer and my servant. It was a summons to me to serve upon a Jury at the forthcoming Sessions of the Central Criminal Court at the Old Bailey. I had never before been summoned on such a Jury, as John Derrick well knew. He believed – I am not certain at this hour whether with reason or otherwise – that the class of Jurors were customarily chosen on a lower qualification than mine, and he had at first refused to accept the summons. The man who served it had taken the matter very coolly. He had said that my attendance or non-attendance was nothing to him; there the summons was; and I should deal with it at my own peril, and not at his.

For a day or two I was undecided whether to respond to this call, or take no notice of it. I was not conscious of the slightest mysterious bias, influence, or

derived: received
occult: supernatural, ghostly
phenomenon: strange occurrence
paper: letter
altercation: fierce argument
customarily: normally

attraction, one way or the other. Of that I am as strictly sure as of every other statement that I make here. Ultimately I decided, as a break in the monotony of my life, that I would go.

The appointed morning was a raw morning in the month of November. There was a dense brown fog in Piccadilly, and it became positively black and in the last degree oppressive East of Temple Bar. I found the passages and staircases of the Court-House flaringly lighted with gas, and the Court itself similarly illuminated. I *think* that, until I was conducted by officers into the Old Court and saw its crowded state, I did not know that the Murderer was to be tried that day. I *think* that, until I was so helped into the Old Court with considerable difficulty, I did not know into which of the two Courts sitting my summons would take me. But this must not be received as a positive assertion, for I am not completely satisfied in my mind on either point.

I took my seat in the place appropriated to Jurors in waiting, and I looked about the Court as well as I could through the cloud of fog and breath that was heavy in it. I noticed a black vapour hanging like a murky curtain outside the great windows, and I noticed the stifled sound of wheels on the straw or tan that was littered in the street; also, the hum of the people gathered there, which a shrill whistle, or a louder song or hail than the rest, occasionally pierced. Soon afterwards the Judges, two in number, entered, and took their seats. The buzz in the Court was awfully hushed. The direction was given to put the Murderer to the bar. He appeared there. And in that same instant I recognised in him the first of the two men who had gone down Piccadilly.

If my name had been called then, I doubt if I could have answered to it audibly. But it was called about sixth or eighth in the panel, and I was by that time able to say 'Here!' Now, observe. As I stepped into the box, the prisoner, who had been looking on attentively, but with no sign of concern, became violently agitated, and beckoned to his attorney. The prisoner's wish to challenge me was so manifest, that it occasioned a pause, during which the attorney, with his hand upon the dock, whispered with his client, and shook his head. I afterward had it from that gentleman, that the prisoner's first

oppressive: smothering
received as a positive assertion: taken as an
   absolute fact
appropriated to: reserved for
tan: tannic acid was spread on busy roads
   to make them less slippery
to the bar: in the dock
box: i.e. the jury box
violently agitated: very upset
attorney: defence counsel
challenge me: try to have me removed
   from the jury
manifest: clear, obvious

COMMENTARY
After some hesitation, the banker attends court to do his duty as a juror. The case which he has to help decide is the 'body in the bedroom' murder. The accused turns out to be the first man that the banker 'saw' in the street.

affrighted words to him were: '*At all hazards, challenge that man!*' But that, as he would give no reason for it, and admitted that he had not ever known my name until he heard it called and I appeared, it was not done.

Both on the ground already explained, that I wish to avoid reviving the unwholesome memory of that Murderer, and also because a detailed account of his long trial is by no means indispensable to my narrative, I shall confine myself to such incidents in the ten days and nights during which we, the Jury, were kept together, as directly bear on my own curious personal experience. It is in that, and not in the Murderer, that I seek to interest my reader. It is to that, and not to a page of the Newgate Calendar, that I beg attention.

I was chosen Foreman of the Jury. On the second morning of the trial, after evidence had been taken for two hours (I heard the church clocks strike), happening to cast my eyes over my brother jurymen, I found an inexplicable difficulty in counting them. I counted them several times, yet always with the same difficulty. In short, I made them one too many.

I touched the brother juryman whose place was next to me, and I whispered to him: 'Oblige me by counting us.' He looked surprised by the request, but turned his head and counted. 'Why,' says he, suddenly, we are Thirt...; but no, it's not possible. No. We are twelve.'

According to my counting that day, we were always right in detail, but in the gross we were always one too many. There was no appearance – no figure – to account for it; but I had now an inward foreshadowing of the figure that was surely coming.

The Jury were housed at the London Tavern. We all slept in one large room on separate tables, and we were constantly in the charge and under the eye of the officer sworn to hold us in safe-keeping. I see no reason for suppressing the real name of that officer. He was intelligent, highly polite, and obliging, and (I was glad to hear) much respected in the City. He had an agreeable presence, good eyes, enviable black whiskers, and a fine sonorous voice. His name was Mr Harker.

When we turned into our twelve beds at night, Mr Harker's bed was drawn

COMMENTARY

The accused recognises the banker amongst the jury and tries to get him replaced. He fails.

Two days into the trial, the banker, who has been made foreman of the jury, counts 13 jurors. There should, of course, only be 12.

hazards: costs
on the ground: for the reason
indispensable: vitally important
in the gross: in total
foreshadowing: premonition
suppressing: concealing
sonorous: loud, booming

across the door. On the night of the second day, not being disposed to lie down, and seeing Mr Harker sitting on his bed, I went and sat beside him, and offered him a pinch of snuff. As Mr Harker's hand touched mine in taking it from my box, a peculiar shiver crossed him, and he said: 'Who is this?'

Following Mr Harker's eyes and looking along the room, I saw again the figure I expected – the second of the two men who had gone down Piccadilly. I rose, and advanced a few steps; then stopped, and looked round at Mr Harker. He was quite unconcerned, laughed, and said in a pleasant way: 'I thought for a moment we had a thirteenth juryman, without a bed. But I see it is the moonlight.'

PAUSE FOR PLAYBACK:

Now look at the playback questions on page 56 before going on with your reading.

Look out for...
- **the growing number of appearances by the murdered man's ghost: what reason might there be for them?**
- **the verdict: is it reached in the right way?**

Making no revelation to Mr Harker, but inviting him to take a walk with me to the end of the room, I watched what the figure did. It stood for a few moments by the bedside of each of my eleven brother jurymen, close to the

not being disposed: not wishing

COMMENTARY

Inside himself, the banker knows who the extra juror is. Sure enough, he 'sees' the second man from Piccadilly in the bedroom which the jurors all share. When the banker's hand touches that of the superintendent of the jury, *he* sees the image too.

pillow. It always went to the right-hand side of the bed, and always passed out crossing the foot of the next bed. It seemed, from the action of the head, merely to look down pensively at each recumbent figure. It took no notice of me, or of my bed, which was the nearest to Mr Harker's. It seemed to go out where the moonlight came in, through a high window, as by an aerial flight of stairs.

Next morning at breakfast, it appeared that everybody present had dreamed of the murdered man last night, except myself, and Mr Harker.

I now felt convinced that the second man who had gone down Piccadilly was the murdered man (so to speak), as if it had been borne into my comprehension by his immediate testimony. But even this took place, and in a manner for which I was not at all prepared.

On the fifth day of the trial, when the case for the prosecution was drawing to a close, a miniature of the murdered man, missing from his bedroom upon the discovery of the deed, and afterwards found in a hiding-place where the Murderer had been seen digging, was put in evidence. Having been identified by the witness under examination, it was handed up to the Bench, and thence handed down to be inspected by the Jury. As an officer in a black gown was making his way with it across to me, the figure of the second man who had gone down Piccadilly impetuously started from the crowd, caught the miniature from the officer, and gave it to me with his own hands, at the same time saying, in a low and hollow tone – before I saw the miniature, which was in a locket – '*I was younger then, and my face was not then drained of blood.*' It also came between me and the brother juryman to whom I would have given the miniature, and between him and the brother juryman to whom he would have given it, and so passed it on through the whole of our number, and back into my possession. Not one of them, however, detected this.

At table, and generally when we were shut up together in Mr Harker's custody, we had from the first naturally discussed the day's proceedings a good deal. On that fifth day, the case for the prosecution being closed, and we having that side of the question in a completed shape before us, our discussion

COMMENTARY

The banker feels a supernatural certainty that the image he keeps seeing is the ghost of the murdered man. Only he can see it. The ghost appears in the jurors' bedroom and is present in court, intervening in the proceedings.

pensively: thoughtfully
recumbent: sleeping
borne into...testimony: made clear to me by the murdered man himself
miniature: small portrait
put: submitted
impetuously started: suddenly jumped to his feet
custody: safe-keeping

was more animated and serious. Among our number was a vestry-man – the densest idiot I have ever seen at large – who met the plainest evidence with the most preposterous objections and who was sided with by two flabby parochial parasites: all the three impanelled from a district so delivered over to Fever that they ought to have been upon their own trial for five hundred Murders. When these mischievous blockheads were at their loudest, which was towards midnight, while some of us were already preparing for bed, I again saw the murdered man. He stood grimly behind them, beckoning to me. On my going towards them, and striking into the conversation, he immediately retired. This was the beginning of a separate series of appearances, confined to that long room in which we were confined. Whenever a knot of my brother jurymen laid their heads together, I saw the head of the murdered man among them. Whenever their comparison of notes was going against him, he would solemnly and irresistibly beckon to me.

It will be borne in mind that down to the production of the miniature, on the fifth day of the trial, I had never seen the Appearance in Court. Three changes occurred now that we entered on the case for the defence. Two of them I will mention together, first. The figure was now in Court continually, and it never there addressed itself to me, but always to the person who was speaking at the time. For instance: the throat of the murdered man had been cut straight across. In the opening speech for the defence, it was suggested that the deceased might have cut his own throat. At that very moment, the figure, with its throat in the dreadful condition referred to (this it had concealed before), stood at the speaker's elbow, motioning across and across its windpipe, now with the right hand, now with the left, vigorously suggesting to the speaker himself the impossibility of such a wound having been self-inflicted by either hand. For another instance: a witness to character, a woman, deposed to the prisoner's being the most amiable of mankind. The figure at that instant stood on the floor before her, looking her full in the face, and pointing out the prisoner's evil countenance with an extended arm and an outstretched finger.

COMMENTARY

As the trial goes on, the murdered man's ghost frequently appears in court as well as in the jurors' bedroom. This is particularly true when there is disagreement between the jurors. He is still seen and heard only by the banker.

animated: intense
vestry-man: vicar
parochial parasites: members of his con-
   gregation who followed him blindly in
   everything
impanelled: called to be jurors
delivered over to Fever: caught up in excitement about the murder trial
retired: disappeared

going against him: pointing to the accused
   being innocent
borne in mind: remembered
deceased: i.e. the murdered man
motioning: making gestures
deposed: gave evidence
most amiable: kindest and gentlest

The third change now to be added impressed me strongly as the most marked and striking of all. I do not theorise upon it; I accurately state it, and there leave it. Although the Appearance was not itself perceived by those whom it addressed, its coming close to such persons was invariably attended by some trepidation of disturbance on their part. It seemed to me as if it were prevented, by laws to which I was not yet amenable, from fully revealing itself to others, and yet as if it could visibly, dumbly, and darkly overshadow their minds. When the leading counsel for the defence suggested the hypothesis of suicide, and the figure stood at the learned man's elbow, frightfully sawing at its severed throat, it is undeniable that the counsel faltered in his speech, lost for a few seconds the thread of his ingenious discourse, wiped his forehead with his handkerchief, and turned extremely pale. When the witness to character was confronted by the Appearance, her eyes most certainly did follow the direction of its pointed finger, and rest in great hesitation and trouble upon the prisoner's face. Two additional illustrations will suffice. On the eighth day of the trial, after a pause which was every day made early in the afternoon for a few minutes' rest and refreshment, I came back into court with the rest of the Jury some little time before the return of the Judges. Standing up in the box and looking about me, I thought the figure was not there, until, chancing to raise my eyes to the gallery, I saw it bending forward, and leaning over a very decent woman, as if to assure itself whether the Judges had resumed their seats or not. Immediately afterwards that woman screamed, fainted, and was carried out. So with the venerable, sagacious and patient Judge who conducted the trial. When the case was over, and he settled himself and his papers to sum up, the murdered man, entering the Judge's door, advanced to his Lordship's desk, and looked eagerly over his shoulder at the pages of his notes which he was turning. A change came over his Lordship's face; his hand stopped; the peculiar shiver, that I knew so well, passed over him; he faltered: 'Excuse me gentlemen, for a few moments. I am somewhat oppressed by the vitiated air,' and did not recover until he had drunk a glass of water.

COMMENTARY

The murdered man's ghost becomes even more active as the trial continues. Although invisible to witnesses and the counsel for the defence, he nevertheless seems able to influence their minds. Even the judge is affected.

theorise: give any explanation
perceived: seen
attended by some trepidation of disturbance: accompanied by signs of alarm
amenable: aware
hypothesis: idea
ingenious discourse: clever speech
venerable: well-respected
sagacious: wise
oppressed: overcome
vitiated: tainted, contaminated

Through all the monotony of six of those interminable ten days – the same Judges and others on the bench, the same Murderer in the dock, the same lawyers at the table, the same tones of question and answer rising to the roof of the Court, the same scratching of the Judge's pen, the same ushers going in and out, the same lights kindled at the same hour when there had been any natural light of day, the same foggy curtain outside the great windows when it was foggy, the same rain pattering and dripping when it was rainy, the same footmarks of turnkeys and prisoner day after day on the same sawdust, the same keys locking and unlocking the same heavy doors – through all the wearisome monotony which made me feel as if I had been Foreman of the Jury for a vast period of time, and Piccadilly had flourished coevally with Babylon, the murdered man never lost one trace of his distinctness in my eyes, nor was he at any moment less distinct than anybody else. I must not omit, as a matter of fact, that I never once saw the Appearance which I call by the name of the murdered man look at the Murderer. Again and again I wondered 'why does he not?' But he never did.

Nor did he look at me, after the production of the miniature, until the last closing moments of the trial arrived. We retired to consider, at seven minutes before ten at night. The idiotic vestryman and his two parochial parasites gave us so much trouble that we twice returned into Court to beg to have certain extracts from the Judge's notes re-read. Nine of us had not the smallest doubt about these passages, neither, I believe, had any one in Court; the dunder-headed triumverate, however, having no idea but obstruction, disputed them for that very reason. At length we prevailed, and finally the Jury returned into Court at ten minutes past twelve.

The murdered man at that time stood directly opposite the jury box, on the other side of the Court. As I took my place, his eyes rested on me with great attention; he seemed satisfied, and slowly shook a great grey veil, which he carried on his arm for the first time, over his head and his whole form. As I gave in our verdict, 'Guilty', the veil collapsed, all was gone, and his place was empty.

interminable: endless
turnkeys: jailers
coevally with Babylon: at the same time as an ancient city renowned for crime and wickedness
to consider: i.e. to reach a verdict
dunder-headed triumverate: stupid trio
obstruction: disagreeing for the sake of it
prevailed: won them over
form: body

COMMENTARY

The banker finds it strange that, throughout the trial, the ghost has never looked at the accused. After 10 days, the jury retire to consider their verdict. The ghost, now covered in a grey veil, instantly vanishes when it is pronounced.

The murderer, being asked by the Judge, according to usage, whether he had anything to say before sentence of Death should be passed upon him, indistinctly muttered something which was described in the leading newspapers of the following day as 'a few rambling, incoherent and half-audible words, in which he was understood to complain that he had not had a fair trial, because the Foreman of the Jury was prepossessed against him.' The remarkable declaration that he really made was this: '*My Lord, I knew I was a doomed man, when the Foreman of my Jury came into the box. My Lord, I knew he would never let me off, because before I was taken, he somehow got to my bedside in the night, woke me, and put a rope around my neck.*'

PAUSE FOR PLAYBACK:
Now look at the playback questions on page 56.

Now look at the playback questions on page 56.

COMMENTARY
The accused protests that he has not had a fair trial. He claims that the banker was biased from the start. More to the point, he accuses the banker of having supernatural powers which he has used against him.

usage: legal custom
incoherent: muddled, unclear
prepossessed: prejudiced
taken: arrested

Study guide

PAGES 43 TO 50:

➤ As soon as the banker reads in his paper a report of the murder, he has a strange experience. What is it exactly? How do you account for it?
➤ Precisely when does John, the banker's servant, see 'a dead man beckoning' (page 47)? Why hasn't he seen it a few seconds before, as the banker has?
➤ Why does the banker immediately recognise the man accused of murder when he steps into the dock at the Old Bailey?
➤ How do *you* explain the fact that the banker believes there are thirteen jurors rather than twelve?

Now return to reading the story on page 50

PAGES 50 TO 55:

➤ The jurors are shown a portrait of the murdered man. Why is this an important piece of evidence for the prosecution? Why is the banker convinced by it?
➤ Does the ghost of the murdered man make an impression only on the banker – or are others affected by it too?
➤ At what point does the murdered man's ghost suddenly disappear? How do you explain this?
➤ After being found guilty, the accused complains that he has not had a fair trial. Do you agree?

REVIEWING THE WHOLE STORY: SUGGESTED ACTIVITIES

1 From beyond the grave

It could be said that the main character in *The Trial for Murder* is not the banker but the ghost of the murdered man. The purpose of this activity is to examine how much influence the ghost has on the events in the story, including the trial itself.

a **With a partner**, draw up a 'ghost's action plan' to show how often, and in what ways, the murdered man's ghost makes sure that he appears to the banker and to others. Set it out like this:

Ghost's action	Effect
1. Produces a picture in the banker's mind of the room in which he was murdered	Makes the banker 'see' the place where he was killed – proves it really happened
2. Appears walking down Piccadilly following his murderer	Fixes both their faces in the banker's mind – shows that he wants revenge
3.	

You should be able to list up to *12* ghost's actions if you look very closely at the story.

b **As a class**, use your completed 'action plan' to discuss:
   - the way in which the ghost's appearances become more frequent, and more influential, as the story goes on.
   - whether the ghost really 'controls' what happens in the story, or whether he is more of a supernatural spectator.

c **In a group**, interview the ghost. Choose up to *six* actions from your list and question him in detail about his purpose in performing them. Take it in turns to play the part of the ghost.

d **By yourself**, write on the following title:

   'In what ways does the ghost of the murdered man attempt to influence the events described in the story? In your opinion, how far does he succeed?'

2 | 'We the jury, find the prisoner...'

The banker tells us that the jury argued for a long time before reaching their verdict. This activity asks you to reconstruct through role-play their discussion of the evidence – and then to reach a verdict.

a   **By yourself**, re-read the paragraph on page 54 beginning 'Nor did he look at me...' The banker – who, remember, is foreman of the jury – says that, in considering their verdict:

> 'The idiotic vestryman and his two parochial parasites gave us so much trouble that we twice returned to Court... [but] ...At length we prevailed...'

Try to imagine what the vicar and his two friends might have said to give the jury 'so much trouble' in making their decision. It is the banker who describes them as 'idiotic': you may think differently.

b   **In a group**, put yourselves in the place of the jury. One person plays the part of the banker, who acts as chairman. There must also be: the vicar; at least one of his 'parasites'; and one or more jurors who think the accused is probably guilty.

Decide who will play which part. Then role-play their discussion of the evidence.

c   Your discussion must be informed by facts. So: skim through the whole story, putting the evidence you find onto a 'proof chart' with three columns, as shown below. Bear in mind two things:

- In law, a man is always presumed innocent until proved guilty.
- You cannot use 'evidence' supplied by a ghost to support your verdict.

Convincing proof of guilt	Possible proof of guilt	Unreliable proof of guilt
1.	1.	1.
2.	2.	2.

Now use your notes to argue your way towards a verdict. There is no reason why *your* verdict should be the same as that reached in the story. It depends on how you, as a group, argue the case.

Your teacher may wish to use this activity to assess your Speaking and Listening skills.

3   The re-trial

Imagine that the accused is allowed a re-trial on the grounds that the banker *was* biased against him – and that, as foreman, he influenced the other jurors to bring in a verdict of 'guilty'.

You are the banker at the re-trial. This time, you are being questioned by the counsel for the defence.

a   **By yourself**, note down the answers you would give *under oath* to the questions below. You *must* use the evidence contained in the story to tell the truth – and only the truth.

> 1. **You claim to have seen the accused walking down Piccadilly from your window. Would you please describe what you saw – and tell the court whether anyone else saw it?**
>
> 2. **When you saw the murdered man beckoning to you from your bedroom door, did your servant, John Derrick, see him too?**
>
> 3. **Would you please describe your state of health in the weeks leading up to the trial?**
>
> 4. **We have heard the evidence of Mr Harker. What do *you* claim to have seen during the night when the jury were staying at the London Tavern – and how do you explain it?**
>
> 5. **You say that the murdered man was continually in court during the giving of evidence. Would you please describe what you saw him doing?**

b   Use your notes to write a confidential letter to the judge at the re-trial. In it you should state (i) whether you still stand by your original verdict or (ii) whether you have now changed your mind. Give detailed reasons for what you say. You are free to refer to other facts mentioned in the story which have not been brought up by the counsel for the defence.

Write your letter in a suitably formal style and in Standard English.

THE HANGED MAN'S BRIDE

Look out for...
- the six 'men in black' who inhabit the house: who do you think they are?
- the old man who speaks to Mr Goodchild and Mr Idle: what is strange about him?
- the fate of Ellen, the 'bride' of the story's title: how does she die?

The house was a genuine old house of a very quaint description, teeming with old carving, and beams, and panels, and having an excellent old staircase, with a gallery or upper staircase, cut off from it by a curious fence-work of old oak, or of the old Honduras Mahogany wood. It was, and is, and will be, for many a long year to come, a remarkably picturesque house; and a certain grave mystery lurking in the depth of the old mahogany panels, as if they were so many deep pools of dark water – such, indeed, as they had been much among when they were trees – gave it a very mysterious character after nightfall.

When Mr Goodchild and Mr Idle had first alighted at the door, and stepped into the sombre handsome old hall, they had been received by half-a-dozen noiseless old men in black, all dressed exactly alike, who glided up the stairs with the obliging landlord and waiter – but without appearing to get into their way, or to mind whether they did or no – and who had filed off to the right and left on the old staircase, as the guests entered the sitting-room. It was then broad, bright day. But, Mr Goodchild had said, when their door was shut,

COMMENTARY
Two friends, Mr Goodchild and Mr Idle, come on holiday to a beautiful country house. As expected, they are greeted by the landlord and his servant. Six other men, each dressed in identical black clothing, also live in the house.

quaint description: unusual and old-fashioned decoration
Honduras Mahogany: finest South American timber
alighted: descended (from a cab)
received: met
whether they did or no: if they did or not

'Who on earth are those old men?' And afterwards, both on going out and coming in, he had noticed that there were no old men to be seen.

Neither had the old men, or any one of the old men, reappeared since. The two friends had passed a night in the house, but had seen nothing more of the old men. Mr Goodchild, in rambling about it, had looked along passages, and glanced in at doorways, but had encountered no old men; neither did it appear that any old men were, by any member of the establishment, missed or expected.

Another odd circumstance impressed itself on their attention. It was, that the door of their sitting-room was never left untouched for a quarter of an hour. It was opened with hesitation, opened with confidence, opened a little way, opened a good way, always clapped-to again without a word of explanation. They were reading, they were writing, they were eating, they were drinking, they were talking, they were dozing; the door was always opened at an unexpected moment, and they looked towards it, and it was clapped-to again, and nobody was to be seen. When this had happened fifty times or so, Mr Goodchild had said to his companion, jestingly: 'I begin to think, Tom, there was something wrong with those six old men.'

Night had come again, and they had been writing for two or three hours: writing, in short, a portion of the lazy notes from which these lazy sheets are taken. They had left off writing, and glasses were on the table between them. The house was closed and quiet. Around the head of Thomas Idle, as he lay upon his sofa, hovered light wreaths of fragrant smoke. The temples of Francis Goodchild, as he leaned back in his chair, with his two hands clasped behind his head, and his legs crossed, were similarly decorated.

They had been discussing idle subjects of speculation, not omitting the strange old men, and were still so occupied, when Mr Goodchild abruptly changed his attitude to wind up his watch. They were just becoming drowsy enough to be stopped in their talk by any such slight check. Thomas Idle, who was speaking at the moment, paused and said, 'How goes it?'

'One,' said Goodchild.

---

establishment: household
impressed itself on their attention: became
   clear to them
jestingly: in a joking way
these lazy sheets: scribbled pages of this
   story
idle subjects of speculation: trivial topics of
   conversation
attitude: position
How goes it?: What's the time?
One: One o'clock in the morning

COMMENTARY
The two friends settle in. They are rather puzzled that they see nothing more of the old men. No one else in the house seems aware of them. Every fifteen minutes, the door of the friends' room opens and closes, though nobody appears at it.

As if he had ordered one old man, and the order were promptly executed (truly, all orders were so, in that excellent hotel), the door opened and one old man stood there.

He did not come in, but stood with the door in his hand.

'One of the six, Tom at last!' said Mr Goodchild, in a surprised whisper. 'Sir, your pleasure?'

'Sir, *your* pleasure?' said the one old man.

'I didn't ring.'

'The bell did,' said the one old man.

He said *bell*, in a deep strong way, that would have expressed the church bell.

'I had the pleasure, I believe, of seeing you, yesterday?' said Goodchild.

'I cannot undertake to say for certain,' was the grim reply of the one old man.

'I think you saw me. Did you not?'

'Saw *you*?' said the old man. 'O yes, I saw *you*. But I see many who never see me.'

A chilled, slow, earthy, fixed old man. A cadaverous old man of measured speech. An old man who seemed as unable to wink, as if his eyelids had been nailed to his forehead. An old man whose eyes – two spots of fire – had no more motion than if they had been connected with the back of his skull by screws driven through it, and riveted and bolted outside, among his grey hair.

The night had turned so cold, to Mr Goodchild's sensations, that he shivered. He remarked lightly, and half apologetically, 'I think somebody is walking over my grave.'

'No,' said the weird old man, 'there is no one there.'

Mr Goodchild looked at Idle, but Idle lay with his head enwreathed in smoke.

'No one there?' said Goodchild.

'There is no one at your grave, I assure you,' said the old man.

He had come in and shut the door, and he now sat down. He did not bend

COMMENTARY

Mr Idle asks the time. On the word 'One', Mr Goodchild's reply, one of the old men appears. He claims Goodchild rang the servant's bell and says he saw him arrive the day before. The old man, who seems barely human, makes Goodchild's blood run cold.

executed: carried out
expressed: suitably described
cadaverous: deadly pale
measured: slow, deliberate
sensations: physical senses

himself to sit as other people do, but seemed to sink bolt upright, as if in water, until the chair stopped him.

'My friend, Mr Idle,' said Goodchild, extremely anxious to introduce a third person into the conversation.

'I am,' said the old man, without looking at him, 'at Mr Idle's service.'

'If you are an old inhabitant of this place,' Francis Goodchild resumed: 'Yes.'

'Perhaps you can decide a point my friend and I were in doubt upon this morning. They hang condemned criminals at the castle, I believe.'

'*I* believe so,' said the old man.

'Are their faces turned towards that noble prospect?'

'Your face is turned,' replied the man, 'to the castle wall. When you are tied up, you see its stones expanding and contracting violently, and a similar expansion and contraction seems to take place in your own head and breast. Then, there is a rush of fire and an earthquake, and the castle springs into the air, and you tumble down a precipice.'

His cravat appeared to trouble him. He put his hand to his throat, and moved his neck from side to side. He was an old man of a swollen character of face, and his nose was immovably hitched up on one side, as if by a little hook inserted in that nostril. Mr Goodchild felt exceedingly uncomfortable, and began to think the night was hot, and not cold.

'A strong description, sir,' he observed.

'A strong sensation,' the old man rejoined.

Again, Mr Goodchild looked to Mr Thomas Idle; but Thomas lay on his back with his face attentively turned towards the one old man, and made no sign. At this time Mr Goodchild believed that he saw threads of fire stretch from the old man's eyes to his own, and there attach themselves. (Mr Goodchild writes the present account of his experience, and, with the utmost solemnity, protests that he had the strongest sensation upon him of being forced to look at the old man along those two fiery films, from that moment.)

'I must tell it to you,' said the old man, with a ghastly and stony stare.

---

decide a point: clear up a question
the castle: an ancient castle stands near to
   the house
tied up: hanging from the noose
cravat: old-fashioned necktie
rejoined: answered
solemnity: seriousness

COMMENTARY
Mr Goodchild questions the old man. He confirms that criminals have always been executed at the nearby castle. The old man seems to know well what it feels like to be hanged.

'What?' asked Francis Goodchild.

'You know where it took place. Yonder!'

Whether he pointed to the room above, or to the room below, or to any room in that old house, or to a room in some other old house in that old town, Mr Goodchild was not, nor is, nor ever can be, sure. He was confused by the circumstance that the right finger of the one old man seemed to dip itself in one of the threads of fire, light itself, and make a fiery start in the air, as if it pointed somewhere. Having pointed somewhere, it went out.

'You know she was a bride,' said the old man.

'I know they still send up bride-cake,' Mr Goodchild faltered. 'This is a very oppressive air.'

She was a bride, said the old man. She was a fair, flaxen-haired, large-eyed girl, who had no character, no purpose. A weak, credulous, incapable, helpless nothing. Not like her mother. No, no. It was her father whose character she reflected.

Her mother had taken care to secure everything to herself, for her own life, when the father of this girl (a child at that time) died – of sheer helplessness; no other disorder – and then he renewed the acquaintance that had once subsisted between the mother and him. He had been put aside for the flaxen-haired, large-eyed man (or nonentity) with money. He could overlook that for money. He wanted compensation in money.

So, he returned to the side of that woman the mother, made love to her again, danced attendance on her and submitted to her whims. She wreaked upon him every whim she had, or could invent. He bore it. And the more he bore, the more he wanted compensation in money, and the more he was resolved to have it.

But, lo! Before he got it, she cheated him. In one of her imperious states, she froze, and never thawed again. She put her hands to her head one night, uttered a cry, stiffened, lay in that attitude certain hours, and died. And he had got no compensation from her in money, yet. Blight and Murrain on her! Not a penny.

COMMENTARY

The old man almost seems able to hypnotise Mr Goodchild. He starts telling him a true story.

There was a woman who married for money, not love. Her husband dies and she becomes rich. She is left with a daughter. Another man, who had been pushed aside in favour of the man she married, begins courting her again.

start: jump
oppressive: close, stifling
credulous: prepared to believe anything
secure everything to herself: make sure she inherited her husband's fortune
disorder: illness
made love to: courted
wreaked upon him: demanded he should give in to
bore: put up with
imperious: domineering, wilful
Blight and Murrain: Plague and Death

He had hated her throughout that second pursuit, and had longed for retaliation on her. He now counterfeited her signature to an instrument, leaving all she had to leave to her daughter – ten years old then – to whom the property passed absolutely, and appointing himself the daughter's Guardian. When he slid it under the pillow of the bed on which she lay, he bent down in the deaf ear of Death, and whispered: 'Mistress Pride, I have determined a long time that, dead or alive, you must make me compensation in money.'

So, now there were only two left. Which two were, he, and the fair flaxen-haired, large-eyed foolish daughter, who afterwards became the bride.

He put her to school. In a secret, dark, oppressive, ancient house, he put her to school with a watchful and unscrupulous woman. 'My worthy lady,' he said, 'here is a mind to be formed; will you help me to form it?' She accepted the trust. For which she, too, wanted compensation in money, and had it.

The girl was formed in the fear of him, and in the conviction, that there was no escape from him. She was taught, from the first, to regard him as her future husband – the man who must marry her – the destiny that overshadowed her – the appointed certainty that could never be evaded. The poor fool was soft white wax in their hands, and took the impression that they put upon her. It hardened with time. It became a part of herself. Inseparable from herself, and only to be torn away from her, by tearing life away from her.

Eleven years she had lived in the dark house and its gloomy garden. He was jealous of the very light and air getting to her, and they kept her close. He stopped the wide chimneys, shaded the little windows, left the strong-stemmed ivy to wander where it would over the house-front, the moss to accumulate on the untrimmed fruit-trees in the red-walled garden, the weeds to over-run its green and yellow walks. He surrounded her with images of sorrow and desolation. He caused her to be filled with fears of the place and of the stories that were told of it, and then on pretext of correcting them, to be left in it in solitude, or made to shrink about it in the dark. When her mind was most depressed and fullest of terrors, then he would come out of one of the hiding-places from which he overlooked her, and present himself as her sole resource.

counterfeited: forged
instrument: legal document
unscrupulous: wicked, without conscience
formed: brought up
evaded: escaped from
close: well-guarded
images: scenes, impressions
pretext: excuse
her sole resource: her only friend and com-
  forter

COMMENTARY
When the woman dies before her suitor can marry her, he is furious. He wanted the money and property her husband left her. But he manages to forge her signature on a will, leaving everything to her 10-year-old daughter. He then makes himself the girl's guardian. His plan is to marry her (and her money) when she is old enough.

Thus, by being from her childhood the one embodiment her life presented to her of power to coerce and power to relieve, power to bind and power to loose, the ascendancy over her weakness was secured. She was twenty-one years and twenty-one days old, when he brought her home to the gloomy house, his half-witted, frightened, and submissive bride of three weeks.

He had dismissed the governess by that time – what he had left to do, he could best do alone – and they came back, upon a rainy night, to the scene of her long preparation. She turned to him upon the threshold, as the rain was dripping from the porch, and said, 'Oh sir, it is the Death-watch ticking for me!'

'Well!' he answered. 'And if it were?'

'O sir!' she returned to him, 'look kindly on me, and be merciful to me! I beg your pardon. I will do anything you wish, if you will only forgive me!'

That had become the poor fool's constant song: 'I beg your pardon,' and 'Forgive me!'

She was not worth hating; he felt nothing but contempt for her. But she had long been in the way, and he had long been weary, and the work was near its end, and had to be worked out.

'You fool,' he said. 'Go up the stairs!'

She obeyed very quickly, murmuring, 'I will do anything you wish!' When he came into the bride's chamber, having been a little retarded by the heavy fastenings of the great door (for they were alone in the house, and he had arranged that the people who attended on them should come and go in the day), he found her withdrawn to the furthest corner, and there standing pressed against the panelling as if she would have shrunk through it: her flaxen hair all wild about her face, and her large eyes staring at him in vague terror.

'What are you afraid of? Come and sit down by me.'

'I will do anything you wish. I beg your pardon, sir. Forgive me!' Her monotonous tune as usual.

COMMENTARY

For eleven years, the girl is kept a prisoner at her guardian's house. He destroys her will and makes her totally dependent on him. When she is 21, he marries her. Now he only has to make sure he will inherit her mother's fortune.

coerce: dictate to
ascendancy: control, domination
governess: home-based teacher
Death-watch: i.e. Death-watch beetle
   (which 'ticks')
retarded: held back, inhibited

'Ellen, here is a writing that you must write out tomorrow, in your own hand. You may as well be seen by others, busily engaged upon it. When you have written it all fairly, and corrected all mistakes, call in any two people there may be about the house, and sign your name to it before them. Then, put it in your bosom to keep it safe, and when I sit here again tomorrow night, give it to me.'

'I will do it all, with the greatest care. I will do anything you wish.'

'Don't shake and tremble, then.'

'I will try my utmost to do it – if you will only forgive me!'

Next day, she sat down at her desk, and did as she had been told. He often passed in and out of the room, to observe her, and always saw her slowly and laboriously writing: repeating to herself the words she copied, in appearance quite mechanically, and without caring or endeavouring to comprehend them, so that she did her task. He saw her follow the direction she had received, in all particulars; and at night, when they were alone again in the same bride's chamber, and he drew his chair to the hearth, she timidly approached him from her distant seat, took the paper from her bosom, and gave it into his hand.

It secured all her possessions to him, in the event of her death. He put her before him, face to face, that he might look at her steadily; and he asked her, in so many plain words, neither fewer nor more, did she know that?

There were spots of ink upon the bosom of her white dress, and they made her face look whiter and her eyes look larger as she nodded her head. There were spots of ink upon the hand with which she stood before him, nervously plaiting and folding her white skirts.

He took her by the arm, and looked her, yet more closely and steadily, in the face. 'Now, die! I have done with you.'

She shrunk, and uttered a low, suppressed cry.

'I am not going to kill you. I will not endanger my life for yours. Die!'

He sat before her in the gloomy bride's chamber, day after day, night after night, looking the word at her when he did not utter it. As often as her large

writing: an official document
before: in front of
endeavouring: attempting
secured: made over, transferred
suppressed: stifled

COMMENTARY
Next day, the bride, Ellen, is given a paper to write out and sign by her guardian-husband. She is so afraid of him that she fails to take in what she is copying. It is, in fact, her will which he has drawn up for her. In it, she leaves everything she owns to him.

unmeaning eyes were raised from the hands in which she rocked her head, to the stern figure, sitting with crossed arms and knitted forehead, in the chair, they read in it 'Die!' When she dropped asleep in exhaustion, she was called back to shuddering consciousness, by the whisper 'Die!' When she fell upon her old entreaty to be pardoned, she was answered 'Die!' When she had out-watched and out-suffered the long night, and the rising sun flamed into the sombre room, she heard it hailed with, 'Another day and not dead? Die!'

Shut up in the deserted mansion, aloof from all mankind, and engaged alone in such a struggle without any respite, it came to this – that either he must die, or she. He knew it very well, and concentrated his strength against her feebleness. Hours upon hours he held her by the arm when her arm was black where he held it, and bade her Die!

It was done, upon a windy morning, before sunrise. He computed the time to be half-past four; but, his forgotten watch had run down, and he could not be sure. She had broken away from him in the night, with loud and sudden cries – the first of that kind to which she had given vent – and he had had to put his hands over her mouth. Since then, she had been quiet in the corner of the panelling where she had sunk down; and he had left her, and had gone back with his folded arms and his knitted forehead to his chair.

Paler in the pale light, more colourless than ever in the leaden dawn, he saw her coming, trailing herself along the floor towards him – a white wreck of hair, and dress, and wild eyes, pushing itself on by an irresolute and bending hand.

'O, forgive me! I will do anything. O, sir, pray tell me I may live!'

'Die!'

'Are you so resolved? Is there no hope for me?'

'Die!'

Her large eyes strained themselves with wonder and fear; wonder and fear changed to reproach; reproach to blank nothing. It was done. He was not at first so sure it was done, but that the morning sun was hanging jewels in her hair – he saw the diamond, emerald and ruby, glittering among it in little points, as he stood looking down at her – when he lifted her and laid her on her bed.

COMMENTARY

During the following days, Ellen's husband never leaves her. He has decided not to risk his own life by murdering her. Instead, he *wills* her to die by repeating, over and over, the command to do so.

unmeaning: vacant
entreaty: plea
aloof: cut off
computed: calculated
irresolute: unsteady
reproach: self-blame

She was soon laid in the ground. And now they were all gone, and he had compensated himself well.

He had a mind to travel. Not that he meant to waste his money, for he was a pinching man and liked his money dearly (like nothing else, indeed), but, that he had grown tired of the desolate house and wished to turn his back on it and have done with it. But, the house was worth money, and money must not be thrown away. He determined to sell it before he went. That it might look the less wretched and bring a better price, he hired some labourers to work in the overgrown garden; to cut out the dead wood, trim the ivy that drooped in heavy masses over the windows and gables, and clear the walks in which the weeds were growing mid-leg high.

He worked, himself, along with them. He worked later than they did, and, one evening at dusk, was left working alone, with his bill-hook in his hand. One autumn evening, when the bride was five weeks dead.

'It grows too dark to work longer,' he said to himself, 'I must give over for the night.'

He detested the house, and was loath to enter it. He looked at the dark porch waiting for him like a tomb, and felt that it was an accursed house. Near to the porch, and near to where he stood, was a tree whose branches waved before the old bay-window of the bride's chamber, where it had been done. The tree swung suddenly, and made him start. It swung again, although the night was still. Looking up into it, he saw a figure among the branches.

It was the figure of a young man. The face looked down, as his looked up; the branches cracked and swayed; the figure rapidly descended, and slid upon its feet before him. A slender youth of about her age, with long light-brown hair.

'What thief are you?' he said, seizing the youth by the collar.

The young man, in shaking himself free, swung him a blow with his arm across the face and throat. They closed, but the young man got from him and stepped back, crying, with great eagerness and horror, 'Don't touch me! I would as lieve be touched by the Devil!'

---

mind: desire
pinching: stingy
determined: made up his mind
bill-hook: sickle, hand-scythe
loath: reluctant
closed: shaped up to fight
as lieve: just as soon

COMMENTARY

Ellen's will to live is finally broken. She dies.

Her husband now has everything he wants. Before heading abroad, he decides to sell the house. He works hard to make the neglected garden look tidy. A young man is watching from a tree.

He stood still, with his bill-hook in his hand, looking at the young man. For, the young man's look was the counterpart of her last look, and he had not expected ever to see that again.

'I am not a thief. Even if I were, I would not have a coin of your wealth, if it would buy me the Indies. You murderer!'

'What!'

'I climbed it,' said the young man, pointing up into the tree, 'for the first time, nigh four years ago. I climbed it, to look at her. I saw her. I spoke to her. I have climbed it, many a time, to watch and listen for her. I was a boy, hidden among its leaves, when from that bay-window she gave me this!'

He showed a tress of flaxen hair, tied with a mourning ribbon.

'Her life,' said the young man, 'was a life of mourning. She gave me this, as a token of it, and a sign that she was dead to every one but you. If I had been older, if I had seen her sooner, I might have saved her from you. But, she was fast in the web when I first climbed the tree, and what could I do then to break it!'

In saying these words, he burst into a fit of sobbing and crying: weakly at first, then passionately, 'Murderer! I climbed the tree on the night when you brought her back. I heard her, from the tree, speak of the Death-watch at the door. I was three times in the tree while you were shut up with her, slowly killing her. I saw her, from the tree, lie dead upon her bed. I have watched you, from the tree, for proofs and traces of your guilt. The manner of it, is a mystery to me yet, but I will pursue you until you have rendered up your life to the hangman. You shall never, until then, be rid of me. I loved her! I can know no relenting towards you. Murderer, I loved her!'

The youth was bare-headed, his hat having fluttered away in his descent from the tree. He moved towards the gate. He had to pass – him – to get to it. There was breadth for two old-fashioned carriages abreast; and the youth's abhorrence, openly expressed in every feature of his face and limb of his body, and very hard to bear, had verge enough to keep itself at a distance in. He (by which I mean the other) had not stirred hand or foot, since he had stood still

COMMENTARY

Ellen's husband threatens him, but is stopped in his tracks when the young man calls him 'murderer'. He loved Ellen. She opened her heart to him, and he knows the reason for her death.

counterpart: exact likeness
nigh: nearly
tress: lock
rendered up: handed over
relenting: feeling of pity
abhorrence: fierce hatred
verge: room

to look at the boy. He faced round, now, to follow him with his eyes. As the back of the bare light brown head was turned to him, he saw a red curve stretch from his hand to it. He knew, before he threw the bill-hook, where it had alighted – I say, had alighted and not would alight; for, to his clear perception the thing was done before he did it. It cleft the head, and it remained there, and the boy lay on his face.

PAUSE FOR PLAYBACK:
Now look at the playback questions on page 81 before going on with your reading.

Look out for...
● **what happens to the young man's corpse.**
● **who the old man telling the bride's story really is.**
● **how Ellen plays an important part in the rest of the story.**

He buried the body in the night, at the foot of the tree. As soon as it was light in the morning, he worked at turning up all the ground near the tree, and hacking and hewing at the neighbouring bushes and undergrowth. When the labourers came, there was nothing suspicious, and nothing suspected.

alighted: landed
to his clear perception: in his mind
cleft: split in two
hewing: chopping

COMMENTARY
The young man swears he will avenge Ellen's death and see her husband brought to justice. The husband is not going to be foiled now. On impulse, he splits open the young man's head with the bill-hook – and kills him outright.

But, he had, in a moment, defeated all his precautions, and destroyed the triumph of the scheme he had so long concerted, and so successfully worked out. He had got rid of the bride, and had acquired her fortune without endangering his life; but now, for a death by which he had gained nothing, he had evermore to live with a rope around his neck.

Beyond this, he was chained to the house of gloom and horror, which he could not endure. Being afraid to sell it or to quit it, lest discovery should be made, he was forced to live in it. He hired two old people, man and wife, for his servants; and dwelt in it, and dreaded it. His great difficulty, for a long time, was the garden. Whether he should keep it trim, whether he should suffer it to fall into its former state of neglect, what would be the least likely way of attracting attention to it?

He took the middle course of gardening himself, in his evening leisure, and of then calling the old serving-man to help him; but, of never letting him work there alone. And he made himself an arbour over against the tree, where he could sit and see that it was safe.

As the seasons changed, and the tree changed, his mind perceived dangers that were always changing. In the leafy time, he perceived that the upper boughs were growing into the form of the young man – that they made the shape of him exactly, sitting in a forked branch swinging in the wind. In the time of the falling leaves, he perceived that they came down from the tree forming tell-tale letters on the path, or that they had a tendency to heap themselves into a churchyard-mound above the grave. In the winter, when the trees were bare, he perceived that the boughs swung at him the ghost of the blow the young man had given, and that they threatened him openly. In the spring, when the sap was mounting in the trunk, he asked himself, were the dried-up particles of blood mounting with it: to make out more obviously this year than last, the leaf-screened figure of the young man, swinging in the wind?

However, he turned his money over and over, and still over. He was in the dark trade, and gold-dust trade, and most secret trades that yielded great

---

COMMENTARY

The husband now feels trapped by the house. Having buried the young man's body under the tree, he needs to watch over it continually. He becomes a recluse, haunted by fear of the body's discovery.

concerted: cleverly planned
an arbour over against the tree: a hide-out made of the tree's branches
perceived: imagined
turned his money: made profits from his investments
dark trade: the Slave Trade

returns. In ten years, he had turned his money over, so many times, that the traders and shippers who had dealings with him, absolutely did not lie – for once – when they declared that he had increased his fortune, twelve hundred per cent.

He possessed his riches one hundred years ago, when people could be lost easily. He had heard who the youth was, from hearing of the search that was made after him; but, it died away, and the youth was forgotten.

The annual round of changes in the tree had been repeated ten times since the night of the burial at its foot, when there was a great thunder-storm over this place. It broke at midnight, and raged until morning. The first intelligence he heard from his old serving-man that morning was, that the tree had been struck by lightning.

It had been driven down the stem, in a very surprising manner, and the stem lay in two blighted shafts: one resting against the house, and one against a portion of the old red garden-wall in which its fall had made a gap. The fissure went down the tree to a little above the earth, and there stopped. There was great curiosity to see the tree, and, with most of his former fears revived, he sat in his arbour – grown quite an old man – watching the people who came to see it.

They quickly began to come, in such dangerous numbers, that he closed his garden-gate and refused to admit any more. But, there were certain men of science who travelled from a distance to examine the tree, and, in an evil hour, he let them in – Blight and Murrain on it, he let them in!

They wanted to dig up the ruin by the roots, and closely examine it, and the earth about it. Never, while he lived! They offered money for it. They! Men of Science, whom he could have bought by the gross, with a scratch of his pen! He showed them the garden-gate again, and locked and barred it.

But they were bent on doing what they wanted to do, and they bribed the old serving-man – a thankless wretch who regularly complained when he received his wages, of being underpaid – and they stole into the garden by night with their lanterns, picks, and shovels, and fell to at the tree. He was

---

intelligence: news
blighted: blasted, split
fissure: deep crack
bent: intent
fell to: started digging

COMMENTARY
Staying in the house does not prevent the husband from making large sums of money by speculating.

One night the tree is struck by lightning. It splits into such a remarkable shape that a group of scientists visits and bribes the gardener to let it dig into its roots.

lying in a turret-room on the other side of the house (the bride's chamber had been unoccupied ever since), but he soon dreamed of picks and shovels, and got up.

He came to an upper window on that side, whence he could see their lanterns, and them, and the loose earth in a heap which he himself had disturbed and put back, when it was last turned to the air. It was found! They had that minute lighted on it. They were all bending over it. One of them said, 'The skull is fractured;' and another, 'See here the bones;' and another, 'See here the clothes;' and then the first struck again, and said, 'A rusty bill-hook!'

He became sensible, next day, that he was already put under a strict watch, and that he could go nowhere without being followed. Before a week was out, he was taken and laid in hold. The circumstances were gradually pieced together against him, and with a desperate malignity, and an appalling ingenuity. But, see the justice of men, and how it was extended to him! He was further accused of having poisoned the girl in the bride's chamber. He, who had carefully and expressly avoided imperilling a hair of his head for her, and who had seen her die of her own incapacity!

There was doubt for which of the two murders he should be first tried; but, the real one was chosen, and he was found guilty, and cast for death. Bloodthirsty wretches! They would have made him guilty of anything, so set they were upon having his life.

His money could do nothing to save him, and he was hanged. *I* am he, and I was hanged at Lancaster Castle with my face to the wall, a hundred years ago!

At this terrific announcement, Mr Goodchild tried to rise and cry out. But, the two fiery lines extending from the old man's eyes to his own, kept him down, and he could not utter a sound. His sense of hearing, however, was acute, and he could hear the clock strike two. No sooner had he heard the clock strike Two, than he saw before him two old men!

Two.

COMMENTARY

The scientists find the bill-hook and the remains of the young man. The husband is accused of his murder and is arrested. Even worse for him, he is also accused of poisoning his bride.

The old man telling the story reveals that *he* is the husband. He was hanged at the nearby castle 100 years before.

turret: tower
whence: from where
sensible: aware
laid in hold: placed under arrest
desperate malignity: awful spite and cunning
expressly: purposely
cast for: sentenced to

The eyes of each, connected with his eyes by two films of fire: each, exactly like the other: each, addressing him at precisely one and the same instant: each, gnashing the same teeth in the same head, with the same twitched nostril above them, and the same suffused expression around it. Two old men. Differing in nothing, equally distinct to the sight, the copy no fainter than the original, the second as real as the first.

'At what time,' said the two old men, 'did you arrive at the door below?'

'At six.'

'And there were six old men upon the stairs!'

Mr Goodchild having wiped the perspiration from his brow, or tried to do it, the two old men proceeded in one voice, and in the singular number:

I had been anatomised, but had not yet had my skeleton put together and re-hung on an iron hook, when it began to be whispered that the bride's chamber was haunted. It *was* haunted, and I was there.

We were there. She and I were there. I, in the chair upon the hearth; she, a white wreck again, trailing itself towards me on the floor. But, I was the speaker no more, and the one word that she said to me from midnight until dawn was 'Live!'

The youth was there, likewise. In the tree outside the window. Coming and going in the moonlight, as the tree bent and gave. He has, ever since, been there, peeping in at me in my torment; revealing to me by snatches, in the pale lights and slaty shadows where he comes and goes bare-headed – a bill-hook, standing edgewise in his hair.

In the bride's chamber, every night from midnight until dawn – one month in the year excepted, as I am going to tell you – he hides in the tree, and she comes towards me on the floor; always approaching, never coming nearer, always visible as if by moonlight, whether the moon shines or no; always saying, from midnight until dawn, her one word, 'Live!'

But, in the month wherein I was forced out of this life – this present month of thirty days – the bride's chamber is empty and quiet. Not so my old

---

suffused: swollen-faced
anatomised: cut up (for medical research)
edgewise: on its edge

COMMENTARY

Mr Goodchild, realising that the old man is a ghost, tries to flee. The clock strikes two. Suddenly, there are *two* identical old men before him. They speak in unison.

The hanged man is under a curse. He is doomed to wander the bride's room as a ghost, taunted by his dead bride with the one word: 'Live!'

dungeon. Not so the rooms where I was restless and afraid, ten years. Both are fitfully haunted then. At one in the morning, I am what you saw me when the clock struck that hour – one old man. At two in the morning, I am two old men. At three, I am three. By twelve at noon, I am twelve old men, one for every hundred per cent of old gain. Every one of the twelve, with twelve times my old power of suffering and agony. From that hour until twelve at night, I, twelve old men in anguish and fearful foreboding, wait for the coming of the executioner. At twelve at night, I, twelve old men turned off, swing invisible outside Lancaster Castle, with twelve faces to the wall!

When the bride's chamber was first haunted, it was known to me that this punishment would never cease, until I could make its nature, and my story, known to two living men together. I waited for the coming of two living men together into the bride's chamber, years upon years. It was infused into my knowledge (of the means I am ignorant) that if two living men, with their eyes open, could be in the bride's chamber at one in the morning, they would see me sitting in my chair.

At length, the whispers that the room was spiritually troubled, brought two men to try the adventure. I was scarcely struck upon the hearth at midnight (I came there as if the lightning blasted me into being), when I heard them ascending the stairs. Next, I saw them enter. One of them was a bold, gay, active man, in the prime of life, some five and forty years of age; the other, a dozen years younger. They brought provisions with them in a basket, and bottles. A young woman accompanied them, with wood and coals for the lighting of the fire. When she had lighted it, the bold, gay, active man accompanied her along the gallery outside the room, to see her safely down the staircase, and came back laughing.

He locked the door, examined the chamber, put out the contents of the basket on the table before the fire – and filled the glasses, and ate and drank. His companion did the same, and was as cheerful and confident as he: though he was the leader. When they had supped, they laid pistols on the table, turned to the fire, and began to smoke their pipes of foreign make.

COMMENTARY

In addition, for one month of the year, the old man has to re-live the horror of being hanged. He is a 'multiple' ghost. At one o'clock, he appears as one old man; at midnight, he appears as twelve. The curse can only be lifted if the hanged man tells his story to two men together. They must hear it in the chamber where the bride died – and their eyes must remain open.

one for every hundred per cent of old gain: the bride's husband made 1200 per cent profit out of her money

together: he must tell his story to *two* men – and they must hear it at the same time

infused into my knowledge: fixed into my mind

gay: lively, cheerful

They had travelled together, and had been much together, and had an
abundance of subjects in common. In the midst of their talking and laughing,
the younger man made a reference to the leader's being always ready for any
adventure; that one, or any other. He replied in these words: 'Not quite so,
Dick; if I am afraid of nothing else, I am afraid of myself.'

His companion seeming to grow a little dull, asked him, in what sense? How?

'Why, thus,' he returned. 'Here is a Ghost to be disproved. Well! I cannot
answer for what my fancy might do if I were alone here, or what tricks my
senses might play, me if they had me to themselves. But, in company with
another man, and especially with you, Dick, I would consent to outface all the
ghosts that were ever told of in the universe.'

'I had not the vanity to suppose that I was of so much importance tonight,'
said the other.

'Of so much,' rejoined the leader, more seriously than he had spoken yet,
'that I would, for the reason I have given, on no account have undertaken to
pass the night here alone.'

It was within a few minutes of one. The head of the younger man had
drooped when he made his last remark, and it dropped lower now. 'Keep
awake, Dick!' said the leader gaily. 'The small hours are the worst.'

He tried, but his head drooped again.

'Dick!' urged the leader. 'Keep awake!'

'I can't,' he indistinctly muttered. 'I don't know what strange influence is
stealing over me. I can't.'

His companion looked at him with a sudden horror, and I, in my different
way, felt a new horror also; for, it was on the stroke of one, and I felt that the
second watcher was yielding to me, and that the curse was upon me that I
must send him to sleep.

'Get up and walk, Dick!' cried the leader. 'Try!'

It was in vain to go behind the slumberer's chair and shake him. One
o'clock sounded, and I was present to the elder man, and he stood transfixed
before me.

---

returned: replied
disproved: shown either to exist or not
fancy: imagination
was yielding to me: was falling under my
    spell

COMMENTARY
When rumours spread that the bride's
chamber is haunted, two ghost-hunters
come to spend the night there. One of
them cannot stop himself from falling
asleep.

To him alone, I was obliged to relate my story, without hope of benefit. To him alone, I was an awful phantom making a quite useless confession. I foresee it will ever be the same. The two living men together will never come to release me. When I appear, the sense of one of the two will be locked in sleep; he will neither see nor hear me; my communication will ever be made to a solitary listener, and will ever be unserviceable. Woe! Woe! Woe!

As the two old men, with these words, wrung their hands, it shot into Mr Goodchild's mind that he was in the terrible situation of being virtually alone with the spectre, and that Mr Idle's immovability was explained by his having been charmed asleep at one o'clock. In the terror of this sudden discovery which produced an indescribable dread, he struggled so hard to get free from the four fiery threads, that he snapped them, after he had pulled them out a great width. Being then out of bonds, he caught up Mr Idle from sofa, and rushed downstairs with him.

'What are you about, Francis?' demanded Mr Idle. 'My bedroom is not down here. What the deuce are you carrying me at all for? I can walk with a stick now. I don't want to be carried. Put me down!'

Mr Goodchild put him down in the old hall, and looked about him wildly.

'What are you doing? Idiotically plunging at your own sex, and rescuing them or perishing in the attempt?' asked Mr Idle, in a highly petulant state.

'The one old man!' cried Mr Goodchild, distractedly, 'and the two old men!'

Mr Idle deigned no other reply than, 'The one old woman, I think you mean,' as he began hobbling his way back up the staircase, with the assistance of its broad balustrade.

'I assure you, Tom,' began Mr Goodchild, attending at his side, 'that since you fell asleep – '

'Come, I like that!' said Thomas Idle, 'I haven't closed an eye!'

With the peculiar sensitiveness on the subject of the disgraceful action of

---

COMMENTARY

The hanged man realises what his *true* curse is: against his will he is doomed to cause one listener's eyes to close. The curse can never be lifted. He must endure being 'alive' and suffering for ever.

Mr Goodchild now understands that his friend, Mr Idle, has been charmed asleep by the hanged man at one o'clock. He has been listening to the story by himself. With a supreme effort, he half drags and half carries Mr Idle out of the bride's chamber — and flees downstairs.

benefit: doing myself any good
sense: mind
ever: always
unserviceable: useless, ineffective
out of bonds: free from the
   hanged man's power
about: up to
petulant: irritable
deigned: took trouble to give
balustrade: banister-rail

going to sleep out of bed, which is the lot of all mankind, Mr Idle persisted in this declaration. The same peculiar sensitiveness impelled Mr Goodchild, on being taxed with the same crime, to repudiate it with honourable resentment. The settlement of the question of the one old man and the two old men was thus presently complicated, and soon made quite impracticable. Mr Idle said it was all bride-cake, and fragments, newly arranged, of things seen and thought about during the day. Mr Goodchild said how could that be, when he hadn't been asleep? Mr Idle said he had never been asleep, and never did go to sleep, and that Mr Goodchild, as a general rule, was always asleep. They consequently parted for the rest of the night, at their bedroom doors, a little ruffled. Mr Goodchild's last words were, that he had had, in that real and tangible old sitting-room of that real and tangible old Inn (he supposed, Mr Idle denied its existence?), every sensation and experience, the present record of which is now within a line or two of completion; and that he would write it out and print it every word. Mr Idle returned that he might if he liked – and he did like, and has now done it.

PAUSE FOR PLAYBACK:
Now look at the playback questions on page 81.

COMMENTARY

Mr Idle continues to deny that he has been asleep. Mr Goodchild knows that he *has*. Thus the only way that Goodchild can 'prove' his experience has been true is to write it down and get it printed. The result is the story of *The Hanged Man's Bride*.

taxed with: accused of
repudiate: deny
impracticable: impossible
ruffled: disturbed, upset
tangible: made of bricks and mortar, not just dreamed up
print it every word: publish all the facts

Study guide

PLAYBACK QUESTIONS

PAGES 61 TO 72:

> ➤ How do you know that the old man telling the bride's story is not human? What do you guess has happened to him?
> ➤ How does the bride's guardian also come, in time, to be her husband? Why is he so intensely cruel to her?
> ➤ 'He detested the house' (page 70). From this point on, what evidence is there that the house becomes like a prison to the bride's husband?
> ➤ Why does the young man get killed? What do you think his murder might lead to later on in the story?

Now return to reading the story on page 72

PAGES 72 TO 80:

> ➤ What is the bride's husband accused of? Is he guilty as charged?
> ➤ The hanged man differs from a 'normal' ghost. In how many ways *is* he different?
> ➤ Do you think that the bride is sufficiently revenged on her husband? Why, or why not?
> ➤ Why will the hanged man never be at rest? Do you think he deserves his fate?

REVIEWING THE WHOLE STORY: SUGGESTED ACTIVITIES

1 Double Murder Charge: a newspaper investigation

'Before a week was out, he was taken and laid in hold' (page 75). This sentence comes from the part of the story describing the husband's arrest for *two* alleged murders. Remind yourself of the relevant facts.

When news of the arrest gets out, it is widely reported in the papers. In this activity your task is to produce a report about it for *The Times*.

a   **With a partner**, note down the information which has led the police to charge the husband with the young man's murder. Solid evidence has been fairly easy for them to establish. From whom will they have got it?

b   On the other hand, the police will have had much more difficulty in 'proving' the bride's murder. The victim has been dead for ten years. Their best eye-witness, the young man, is also dead. Up to now, the husband has not been suspected. They cannot trace the governess.

In fact, the police have decided that their best hope is to force a confession from the husband. **In a group**, role-play their interrogation of him. Decide who plays the part of the husband. Other members of your group are police interrogators.

Remember that the husband did *not*, in the normal sense of the word, 'murder' his young bride. Will he still confess to causing her death?

c   **With a partner**, act out the two interviews you, as a *Times* reporter, have with the police officer leading the double murder enquiry. One of these centres on the husband's alleged murder of the young man. The other is about the husband's alleged murder of the bride. Take it in turns to play the reporter and the police officer.

d   **By yourself**, plan and write your article. Think carefully about the 'angle' you are going to use. Are you happy simply to report what the police officer has told you – or do you suspect that justice is not fully being done? It is entirely up to you to decide how to construct the article and what to say in it.

Your teacher will advise you about the *style* in which to write.

2 | 'Die! Die! Die!' ... 'Live! Live! Live!'

In *The Hanged Man's Bride*, the husband drives Ellen to her death partly as a way of taking revenge against her parents – especially her mother. Ellen gets her revenge on her husband by haunting him – although he is dead!

This activity asks you to consider who suffers the most pain and anguish during the course of the story: the bride or her husband.

a   **In a group**, divide yourself equally between those who are going to argue that the bride suffers more and those who will argue the opposite. There is strong evidence for both points of view. For the moment, you may have to put aside what you 'really think'. The point of the activity is for you to assemble convincing evidence for your case and to argue it well.

b   Spend half an hour scanning the story for points to support your argument. Make notes and discuss the story with other people who are on your 'side'. Then spend a further half hour conducting your debate.

Your teacher may wish to use this activity to assess your Speaking and Listening skills.

3 | A ghastliness of ghosts

There is a total of 14 ghosts in this story (at least, when the clock strikes midnight) – which may well be a literary record. This activity asks you to judge how good a ghost story *The Hanged Man's Bride* is by expressing your own opinions about it.

a   **As a class**, discuss the typical 'ingredients' of ghost stories. Refer to films and videos you have seen as well as to other published writings.
    Compare them with *The Hanged Man's Bride* by asking:
    - how many typical 'ghostly' ingredients does Dickens's story have?
    - in how many ways does it *differ* from most stories of the supernatural?

b   **With a partner**, work out exactly how many people in the story are being haunted, at some stage or other, by drawing a 'ghost chain' like this:

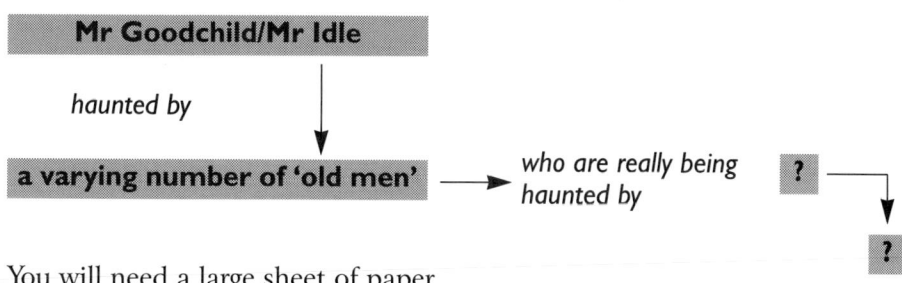

You will need a large sheet of paper.

c   **In a group**, talk about whether Dickens has introduced too many 'layers' of ghosts and hauntings into the story – or whether this makes for an original and intriguing plot. Say what you really think.

One way of testing out your opinion is to imagine *The Hanged Man's Bride* as a film. If you had the task of directing it, how would you make clear what was going on? Could it be made frightening – or would it simply end up by being rather silly?

d   **By yourself**, give your views about *The Hanged Man's Bride* by writing on the following title:

> 'How does Dickens try to make *The Hanged Man's Bride* an original and unusual ghost story? Say, with reasons, whether he succeeds.'

4 | The young man's story

Remind yourself of the part played in this story by the young man, both when he is alive and after his death.

a   **In a group**, refer to the text to build up your ideas about how his relationship with Ellen might have developed. How did he come to know of her, and of her plight? Why did she confide her troubles in him? Why did he fall in love with her?

b   **With a partner**, consider how the young man's ghost influences events in the second half of the story. Decide how important he is in bringing Ellen's husband to justice.

c   **By yourself**, write *The Young Man's Story*. You can do this *either* as a commentary *or* by putting yourself in the young man's place and writing in his own words.

Overview

The activities in this section ask you to do two things:

1   Talk and/or write about the stories in order to understand more about the way they are told.

    You will be looking at:

    - **Narrative**   The way a story is built up and organised.

    - **Characterisation**   The way the characters are presented to us.

    - **Themes**   The main ideas and issues the author writes about.

    - **Setting and atmosphere**   The importance of particular places and how they are described in a story.

2   Make comparisons between some of the stories.

1 Performing the stories: rehearsed readings

By yourself, choose passages from two of the stories in this volume to read aloud. Your teacher may wish to make this into a Speaking and Listening (Performance) assignment on which you can be assessed, either for Key Stage 3 or for GCSE Oral Coursework.

Advice (i) – Selecting

- Some passages will 'perform' better than others, so your choice is important. It can be entirely yours. If you want some guidance, the following passages would be suitable:

  - from *The Signalman*, the passage running from 'Punctual to my appointment...' (page 15) to '"All well"' (page 16).

  - from *Confession Found in a Prison*, the passage running from 'Hard by our cottage' (page 33) to 'his cheek resting upon his little hand' (page 34).

  - from *The Trial for Murder*, the passage running from 'The appointed morning' (page 48) to 'it was not done' (page 49).

  - from *The Hanged Man's Bride*, the passage running from 'She was not worth hating' (page 67) to '"I will not endanger my life for yours. Die!"' (page 68).

Advice (ii) – Rehearsing and performing

- Read the passage slowly to yourself. Check in the glossary any words or phrases that are unclear. Try to 'hear' the voice of the narrator and the voices of the characters in your head.

- Try reading just *one* paragraph onto tape, in private. Play it back and be *constructively* self-critical. Try again. You will almost certainly have read too fast the first time. The more slowly you read, the more expressive you will sound.

- By the time you come to perform 'for real' – either onto tape or live – you should know your passage very well, as if you were appearing in a play. This will give you more confidence than anything else. It is a good idea to have a photocopy so that you can (i) underline words that you want to emphasise (ii) make vertical strokes where you need to pause.

- As you perform, put this formula into practice:

  Getting the meaning across really well } **the right tone + varying the pace as you go + clarity of speech**

2 Haunted characters

In all four stories in this volume, characters are haunted – sometimes by fear, sometimes by their past, sometimes by guilt, sometimes by evil...and so on.

By yourself, compare the way in which any two characters are haunted. Show clearly what it is they are haunted *by* – and for what reasons.

Points to consider

- Ghosts can appear in many shapes and forms. In the stories you have chosen, think about the following:

    - How does the character concerned first become aware of being haunted?

    - What feelings is the haunted character made to experience by 'his' ghost?

    - What is the ghost trying to achieve?

    - What do you think the ghost represents?

- In *The Signalman*, how do the story's descriptions show that the railway cutting (i.e. landscape, the tunnel, the red light, etc.) reflects the nature of the ghost?

- In *Confession Found in a Prison*, what is the importance of the blood-hounds to the 'revenge' theme of the story? Why does Dickens choose them?

- In *The Trial for Murder*, do you think that the ghost achieves justice for itself – or is it just playing a confidence trick?

- In *The Hanged Man's Bride*, are we made to feel any pity for the ghost of the dead husband – or does he deserve his suffering?

Suggestions for writing

a   How do any *two* characters in different stories suffer from being haunted? In your view, which suffers the more?

b   'Dickens wrote about the supernatural merely to entertain us rather than to explore serious themes.' Show how far you agree with this statement by considering at least *two* stories.

3 | In suspense

The stories in this volume all depend on *suspense* for their effectiveness.

As a class, or **in groups**, discuss *two or more* of them to decide how well Dickens manages to 'keep us guessing'. Your teacher may wish to use this activity to assess your Speaking and Listening skills.

Points to consider

- In *The Signalman*, do you think the following increase the suspense of the story:
  - the use of the story-teller as a character rather than an 'unseen' third-person narrator?
  - the repetition of the same pattern of events?
  - the way in which the signalman *gradually* reveals his experiences?

- In *Confession Found in a Prison*, does the narrator:
  - spoil the suspense by telling us straight away that he is going to be executed?
  - add to the suspense by not giving a clear motive for killing the boy?
  - manage to keep from us until the end the *way* in which he is caught?

- In *The Trial for Murder*, how successfully does the banker keep us in suspense by:
  - not bringing out the identity of the ghost until part way through the story?
  - making us wonder whether he is *wrongly* guided by the ghost?
  - leaving the fairness of the verdict in doubt at the end of the story?

- In *The Hanged Man's Bride*, how much suspense is aroused by:
  - the mystery of the 'one old man and the twelve old men'?
  - the sudden appearance half-way through the story of the young man?
  - the story about the 'curse' which the ghost tells Mr Goodchild?

These questions are meant to give you some starting-points. Ask your *own* questions too, and follow your own agenda on the subject of suspense.

4 | Film sets

As a class, or **in groups**, discuss how you would go about filming *one* or *two* of these stories. Concentrate most on the 'sets' you would use.

Points to consider

- In *The Signalman*:
  - how would you establish the mood or atmosphere of your film in the opening few shots?
  - much of the story consists of the signalman talking in his box to the narrator, which could be boring on film. How would you get round this?
  - what would you show in the closing shots of your film? With what feelings would you want to leave the viewer?

- In *Confession Found in a Prison*:
  - what would the prison cell look like, exactly? What appearance would you want the murderer to have at the start of your film?
  - how would you build up the murderer's feeling of fear after he has buried the boy's body?
  - how would you film the ending where the murderer is caught? Would you want to make it like part of a horror film? Why, or why not?

- In *The Trial for Murder*:
  - what are the main locations you would have to use in the film? How would you bring out the differences between them?
  - how would you film the appearances of the ghost in such a way as to prevent it from seeming comic?
  - what would you want to happen in the courtroom after the accused speaks the final words of the story?

- In *The Hanged Man's Bride*:
  - how would you convey the atmosphere of the old house at the start of the film?
  - what feeling would you want to build up when the husband is 'willing' his bride to die? How would you do it?
  - would you make any use in your film of the old castle where the husband was hanged? If so, where would you introduce it?

By yourself, write the director's notes for a film of at least *one* of these stories. Choose to write about the things *you* think would be most important to the success of your film(s).

5 Comparing and judging

As a class, or **in groups**, compare *two* of these stories in order to make a personal judgement about which one is the more enjoyable and effective.

Points to consider

- **Plot** Ask yourselves:

    - how skilfully is the story as a whole 'shaped' or constructed?

    - is the action too drawn-out – or does it move along at a pace that holds your interest?

    - are the events sufficiently original – or do they seem like re-workings of old ideas?

    - do the 'twists and turns' in the story take you by surprise – or are they too predictable?

- **Characters** Ask yourselves:

    - does the author make you care about his characters? Do they arouse strong feelings in you?

    - are the relationships between the characters true-to-life and convincing – or do they seem false?

    - are the characters *consistent* all the way through the story – or do they behave inconsistently?

- **Style** Ask yourselves:

    - is the story written in a way that is well suited to what it is about?

    - what do you think of the balance between the author's description and the dialogue (that is, characters speaking)?

These questions are intended to focus your discussion. There are other aspects of the stories you may want to consider.

By yourself, write a comparison between any *two* stories from this volume, saying, with reasons, which you enjoyed the more.